THE JOURNEY

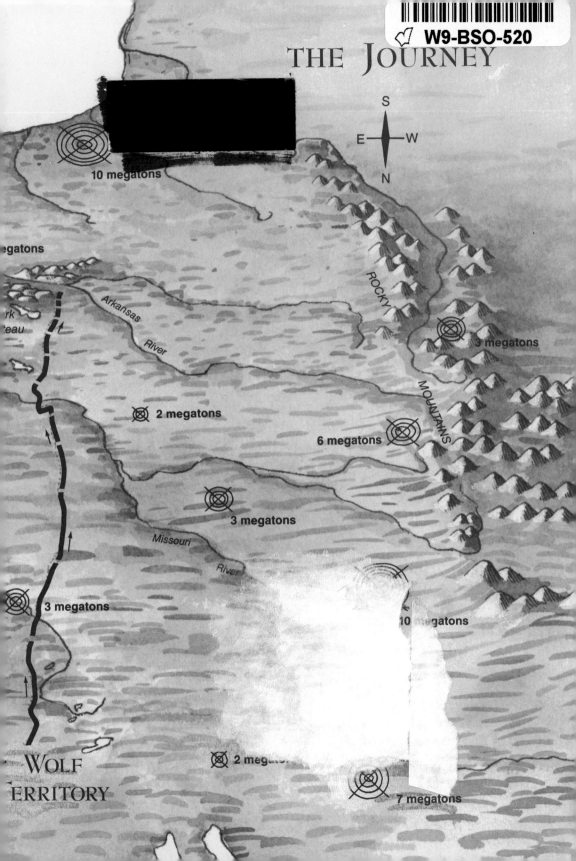

S

E ✦ W

N

10 megatons

...egatons

ROCKY

Arkansas

River

3 megatons

rk
teau

2 megatons

6 megatons

MOUNTAINS

3 megatons

Missouri

River

10 megatons

3 megatons

WOLF
ERRITORY

2 mega...

7 megatons

WOLF OF SHADOWS

WOLF
OF SHADOWS

by Whitley Strieber

Alfred A. Knopf · New York

Sierra Club Books · San Francisco

THIS IS A BORZOI BOOK PUBLISHED BY ALFRED A. KNOPF, INC.

Copyright © 1985 by Wilson & Neff, Inc.
Jacket illustration copyright © 1985 by Marc Rosenthal
All rights reserved under International and Pan-American Copyright
Conventions. Published in the United States by Alfred A. Knopf, Inc.,
New York, and simultaneously in Canada by Random House of
Canada Limited, Toronto. Distributed by Random House, Inc., New York.
Designed by Eileen Rosenthal. Manufactured in the
United States of America   10 9 8 7 6 5 4 3 2 1

Library of Congress Cataloging in Publication Data
Strieber, Whitley. Wolf of Shadows.
Summary: In the terrible aftermath of a nuclear holocaust, a wolf
and a human woman form a mysterious bond that brings each
close to the spirits of the shattered earth.
[1. Wolves—Fiction. 2. Nuclear warfare—Fiction.
3. Survival—Fiction]   I. Title.
PZ7.S91675Wo   1985   [Fic]   84-20133
ISBN 0-394-87224-X   ISBN 0-394-97224-4 (lib. bdg.)

Map by David Lindroth

Grateful acknowledgment is made to the John G. Neihardt Trust for permission to reprint an excerpt from *Black Elk Speaks* by John G. Neihardt. Copyright © 1932 by John G. Neihardt, renewed 1959. Published by the University of Nebraska Press.

The Sierra Club, founded in 1892 by John Muir, has devoted itself to the study and protection of the earth's scenic and ecological resources—mountains, wetlands, woodlands, wild shores and rivers, deserts and plains. The publishing program of the Sierra Club offers books to the public as a nonprofit educational service in the hope that they may enlarge the public's understanding of the club's basic concerns. The point of view expressed in each book, however, does not necessarily represent that of the club. The Sierra Club has some fifty chapters coast to coast, in Canada, Hawaii, and Alaska. For information about how you may participate in its programs to preserve wilderness and the quality of life, please address inquiries to Sierra Club, 730 Polk Street, San Francisco, CA 94109.

*This book is dedicated to the hope
that children and wolves have a future.*

ACKNOWLEDGMENTS

Wolf of Shadows could not have
been completed without the faith and
support of Douglas Hardy
of Knopf/Pantheon Books for Young Readers.
I am also indebted to T.C. McLuhan
for her book *Touch the Earth,* in which
I found much wisdom.

PART ONE

The Lost Spring

The old Lakota was wise. He knew that man's heart away from nature becomes hard; he knew that lack of respect for living, growing things soon led to lack of respect for humans too.

Chief Luther Standing Bear

HE WAS A GIANT of his kind; he had been the biggest of his litter and he had stayed much larger than the other wolves. He was black and had pale eyes, and from an early age he made the others uneasy. He was never accepted, and was driven to live at the edge of the pack. Because he was dark and spent his life hanging back in the forest, he was Wolf of Shadows.

When the pack howled together his loneliness would become acute, and he would draw close to them, his tail down, his ears cocked to hear any hostile growl.

It had not always been like this. Once he had been part of a litter. He had enjoyed his mother's warmth, had tussled with his littermates. He remembered playing in the sun.

Things changed, though. When he began to pass into maturity other young males had started challenging him. He did not want to fight; he wanted to have a place in the pack. Sometimes he was forced to accept the offered battles; often, though, he turned away, and went off to wait for the others to settle.

In time he became a huge creature, fierce from all the discord, his head high, his tail waving proudly.

The old pack leader, uneasy with him, demanded that he submit. His heart would not let him; neither, though, would he fight the pack leader, for he knew that the outcome would make him alpha wolf, and he did not think the others would let him lead them.

The wise old leader saw that there was an impasse and struck a nervous truce: He would ignore Wolf of Shadows if the giant ignored him.

Seasons passed, and a time came when a powerful young gray challenged the old leader and eagerly became alpha wolf. He was quick and strong, and his flashing jaws humbled the wolves who tested him. At last there was only one wolf who had not fought—the huge black who now lived in the forest.

He stood almost a head above the gray, and all the wolves knew that he could certainly beat him. Because of this imbalance the gray could not become firm leader. No wolf was content in his place: The young fought the old, and even females were in contention. There was no place in the gray's taut hierarchy for the big wolf, not even at the edge.

Wolf of Shadows might not wish to lie with the others, but he had never been warned away from the hunt. He chased the deer and the moose with them, sharing the blood of their kills.

Now the pack denied the proud black giant his last connection with them. When he ran to the hunt, they showed him their teeth. They had never done this before. If he could not hunt with them, nor lie among them afterward gorged and sleepy, he would be truly alone. He would never be licked, nor touch other wolves.

He mewed like a cub. But he did not roll to the gray and so he was banished. He withdrew farther into the woods, remaining almost out of scent of the pack, wandering long hours alone at the very limit of its most distant marks.

The season grew older, and when the first flowers came through the snow there was a change in his body. His loins ached; he found himself under an almost unbearable compulsion. Day by day he moved closer to the pack. When he scented the young females, his flesh grew warm with longing.

He emerged into the full light of the lakeshore where the pack lived. There he hesitated, a big-footed young wolf, his eyes bright and his tongue dangling from the side of his mouth.

To the pack he was almost a stranger. Some of the younger wolves hardly knew him at all. The others watched him, ears back, tails down. Some snarled. Growling, the gray ran at him. Wolf of Shadows could not react, not without risking a fight in which he would almost certainly beat the alpha wolf. Whining, he went back into the forest.

By day he remained near them, carefully avoiding the nervous challenges of the gray and scenting the graceful odors of the females—especially the gray's, the one with the gentle pride in her gaze. She was the one he most wanted to nuzzle and smell.

At night, after the crickets and frogs slept and the fireflies had settled in the grass, he remained awake, battling his own urges. His body demanded that he rub against the females, that he sniff them, that he climb their backs. Days and nights passed, and spring filled the air with new scents, but Wolf of Shadows hardly noticed. He was interested only in the females, some young and sweet, others heavy with the memory of many litters.

His need grew and grew, until his body quivered with it. At night he would leap up, his heart thundering, his nose questing for a female who wasn't there. Through the small hours he would remain awake, pacing at the limits of the pack's range. It was only a question of time before his desires would make him wild.

At last, in a desperate attempt to control himself, he began to run. He went without sense or direction, far from the pack's territory, passing beneath the oak and the sycamore, not stopping until the wind of dawn rose in the pines.

The world that sunrise spread before his senses was transformed, the new buds shining with dew, the warblers and the jays jumping eagerly. He drew into his muzzle the rich changes of dawn, and for the first time in many a season did not smell wolf scent.

It was a relief. The absence of female odors had a powerful calming effect on his body. He seemed to smell the world anew. He tasted each breath as if it were the only and the last. As he sensed the vibrant maze of humid and dry, cool and hot, frozen and wet, sensed the smell of hidden animals, their fur and their flesh, the dank breath of rats and beavers, sensed the smoothness of the light itself, he found something that for him would remain true for a long time: The way for him to be content was to go far from the land and ways of other wolves, to be alone.

From then on his days were solitary. He slept, he hunted small animals, he scavenged. He went far beyond the pack's scent marks. The deeper he went into the woods, the richer the odors of life became. In the darkest places, where the owls swooped low in the night and the bears grumbled, he could almost forget the pack.

He became a curious creature, every day finding rich new odors. Finally there was only one place near the lake country he had not been, and it was a most dangerous place.

The idea of entering the territories of man made him flatten his ears and lower his tail. But then he would catch a human scent, so strange, so interesting, that he would find himself wandering a little closer to the long, straight paths and the human places.

Before he knew it, he was deep in man's lands. He moved by night, curling during the day in deep underbrush, barely sleeping, alert to every strange sound and smell around him. To comfort himself it was his habit to fill the long nights with the sound of his own voice. Soon his howl was heard in the little towns beyond the water country.

One night there came a smell of dogs, then a sound of rhythmic panting. He smelled spittle and hot breath, and knew they were hunting him, and men were with them. But he did not retreat. The fascinating new odors drew him farther.

Humanity did not have one smell, but many. There were the sharp, lifeless odors of things, the ones that rolled on thick round paws, roaring and snarling as they went down the straight paths. The things that soared, huge shrieking birds, made Wolf of Shadows cringe and left a sweet, hot smell that sifted from the sky. Others did not move but blazed with light and stank of burned meat, and men went into them, and could be seen behind walls of hard air, eating the black meat in the strange dens.

Wolf of Shadows could only conclude that the things themselves led the great human pack—dragged the men from place to place, made them move even more than thirsty rats in the autumn, and made all these eerie smells, so lifeless and yet so full of the heat of activity.

As he crept in the shadows at the edge of the human territories, making dogs bark and causing men to be dragged after him by fiery eyes that had attached themselves to their forepaws, he sensed the danger increasing. Then, one night, he heard the bark of a death-stick, a thing he had learned to fear, for he had seen the death-stick spit sparks that tore wolves apart.

He recognized that he would soon be brought to

ground if he did not leave, and so he returned to the water country.

Months passed, then seasons and years. His loneliness directed him back to the simple scents he had first known—grass and trees, and the crackling sharpness of an autumn stream.

He was close enough to his old pack to keep track of kills he might scavenge, but not so close that the wolf scent would disturb him. By now he had reached an accommodation with them. Both he and the gray tolerated each other as long as neither came too close.

One evening during the season of the unfolding of leaves he was sitting on his favorite bald hill, his ears erect, sniffing the subtle changes that evening brought to the air about him. Darkness had only just come crawling out from under the rocks—had hardly begun its climb up the sky—when a series of brilliant white flashes drew him to focus his eyes and stare upward.

Although much of the animal world saw the flashes, most creatures ignored them. The owl who lived in the pines preened her wings, preparing for the dance she danced nightly with the water rats. Beneath her a fox sniffed after a hurrying beetle. A water rat awoke and began staring through eyes that reflected but did not really see the darting flames high above. The rat searched the sky, but only for something important: the swift shape of the owl.

Wolf of Shadows shook himself. The bright streaks were very, very wrong. They were like moonbeams, straight and quick and silver, but they were not in the lake and there was no moon. There were no unusual odors, but he felt that the streaks had a scent as cold as winter stones.

In his heart he also heard the streaks hissing like the icy wind that slips winter beneath the warmest coat.

Wolf of Shadows crouched low, growling softly, feeling the spring breeze stir his short hairs. From the bottom of the hill the pack wolves watched him curiously.

The streaks began to fade, becoming as faint as spiderwebs shot with dawn, then disappeared over the horizon.

At once a huge light mushroomed up from where they had gone. Wolf of Shadows turned away from the light and saw his shape sharply outlined against grass made white-silver by the glare.

A boiling, flaring cloud was rising from the human territories. Its light fired the evening sky like dawn. The larks, which had been spiraling down toward the trees, now began to rise again, lured by this false morning.

The pack had drawn close together. Their breath mingled, and their muzzles shook with the effort to scent the cause of the turmoil.

From his hilltop Wolf of Shadows could already see the glare of the fires that had started burning in the human lands. He lowered his tail, laid back his ears, and crept down toward the other wolves.

His sensitive footpads knew the language of the ground, and it was beginning to speak in an unaccustomed way. Something was rushing up through the earth, a great disturbance. The rest of the pack now felt it too, and the other wolves began to whine. The foxes barked and the water rats dove into their pond. Clutching her perch, the owl turned her head about. The moths began to flutter more rapidly, and sleeping day birds fluffed their feathers. Mice and shrews ran, and the lake resounded with the splashes of fish.

There was a sharp shock, followed by a series of smaller ones. Wolf of Shadows could sense deep vibrations. A tickle along his spine made him shudder.

Then night reasserted itself. The owl went back to hunting and the rats to hiding, and the fox to his kit, who began to lick him. The wolf cubs came out beneath the sky.

Wolf of Shadows heard, on the next lake, the human hunters who came every summer muttering nervously in their camp. Their voices were as tight as vines twisting in air.

With each breath he drew, Wolf of Shadows became more disturbed. Again and again he sniffed, seeking for the stillness that had always been behind the murmuring scents of the world. But that special calm was no longer there. Where it had been there was now something else, a smell full of heat. The horizon was filled with fire.

He put his ears back, then barked an alarm. The pack wolves reacted, inhaling sharply. They pricked their ears toward him in question. He threw back his head and howled high. His call made the whole pack raise their muzzles and howl. Their voices echoed across the lake, silencing the loons and the crickets. Other wolves took up the call, and it spread through all the packs of the water country.

Wolf of Shadows howled with such passion, his whole body trembling from it, that even the cubs began to whine.

He loped nearer to the pack than he had been in a very long time. He stopped, and stared straight at the gray. Staring back, the pack leader growled a confused warning. The normally shy loner had broken the rule.

When Wolf of Shadows came even closer, the gray growled loudly. His young wolves came up, their teeth gleaming in the faint light. But Wolf of Shadows did not withdraw. Soon the fire would enter the water country. He raised his head and set forth his howl again, filling it with powerful bell-tones of command. There was no reaction. He used the signals of warning, the sharp bark, the flash of the tail, the hackles raised.

The gray cocked his ears toward the giant wolf, but he did not move. It was clear that neither the gray nor his pack realized the danger in the south. Wolf of Shadows could not make any of them run. There was no way to make them climb his hill, to smell what he had smelled. He thought of escaping alone, the wind rushing up his muzzle, his paws finding the soft places in the path to safety. But they were his pack, his blood and being. He could not leave them, and yet he did not want to burn. The conflict confused him and made him break his gaze. At once the gray turned away. The confrontation over, the pack lost interest.

Wolf of Shadows watched them settle. The world suddenly seemed very large. The darkness beneath the trees had never been more dense, nor the air more full of menace. He would have to decide between the terror of the fire and his loyalty to the wolves.

He went back to his hilltop. The odor that greeted him

now was a shock. His skin felt cold, his withers shook, he snorted out the slick stink that was pouring up from the human territories. The horizon glittered like the eyes of a raging she-bear. Above its edge there was a tremendous cloud, as black as the inner depths of a lake.

The cloud boiled in fury. It was hate unbound—not the struggling rage of an animal trapped by the human hunters' agony-jaws, nor the anguish of a mouse wriggling on a hungry tongue, but something else, a steaming, clotted malevolence that killed all and killed indifferently, humbling everything from mayfly to man.

Even though the odors from the valley were still subtle, they were so oily from burning flesh that Wolf of Shadows blew to get them out of his muzzle. The urge to run became overwhelming, but just as he was about to obey it, the scent of the pack came wafting up from the lake.

He perceived the gray innocently curled up in sleep, and around him the males, the females, the cubs. They had never known anything beyond their range. They felt powerful and safe. Only a wanderer could know how small and frail they really were. In their odor he smelled slow breath and sleep. He could not leave them, no matter what it meant. He whined, soft and low, then sat down to wait with the wolves.

He had not been waiting long when another scent intruded, one that no wolf would ever ignore: the smell of men. A quick flick of his ears disclosed sharp human growling from the next lake over: the hunters were huddling around a little fire, their scents now musky with fear, their growling full of cries. When the sky flickered white and shouted again, the hunters screamed like wolves with their paws caught in agony-jaws.

The sound quickened Wolf of Shadows' blood. Wolves thought of humans as strong. The sound of their fear made him draw his ears back. If they were afraid, wolves should be even more afraid.

The wind hissed in the grass of the bald hill. He looked down toward the other wolves. To save them he would have to try to force himself on them. He whined, then rolled on the ground, covering himself with comforting dust.

When he stopped and sniffed the air again, the scent of a certain female entered his muzzle. He inhaled more avidly. Before he had become a wanderer, he had scented her, that soft, proud wolf, the gray's mate. His heart pounded. He had always wanted that wolf and he wanted her now, with his nose and his tongue and his loins—she whose voice sounded like fast water, who was slow to withdraw from the caress of a loving muzzle. If he took the pack she would be his mate, and become wide with his cubs.

He would sit then as the gray often sat, his muzzle pointing at the sky, his voice rising with contentment. But what then of the gray? He would live a humiliated life at the edge of the pack, or he would die. The gray was strong and good and ought to be left alone.

In the south the cloud was growing into a flying mountain. Even the ring of the crickets had changed, and Wolf of Shadows now scented an uglier smell than any that had come before, the unmistakable smell of fire in treetops. The southern edge of the forest had started burning.

Behind him fingers of clouds were uncurling across the heavens with unnatural speed. The sky grew blacker and blacker. In their camp, the hunters began to shriek. Their brittle stench told him that they were now almost crazy with fear.

He ran along the edge of the hill, hardly able to look at the turmoil that covered half the sky. Finally, he turned and went back down toward the still lake, and the pack. Here there was as yet no scent of burning; that smell had not yet come down from the high places.

He came to a place where he sometimes stayed when the pack was at the lake. His own scent was strong in this copse, and his body had matted the foliage down. He was tingling, full of passion, excited. His decision was made: He would take the pack and lead it to safety.

PART TWO

The Exiles

It was lonesome, the leaving. Husband dead, friends dead ... Strong men, well women, and little children killed ... They had not done wrong to be so killed. We had only asked to be left in our own homes, the homes of our ancestors. Our going was with heavy hearts, broken spirits ... All lost, we walked silently into the wintry night.

Wetatonmi, during the exile of the Nez Percé

WOLF OF SHADOWS ran toward the pack, his breath coming faster and faster, his mind full of the smells and sounds of the fight he knew must come.

Then he heard a noise, faint but unusual enough to make him stop. He became still, pricking his ears toward the sky. It was the droning of a bird-thing of the kind that sometimes lit like a huge goose on the lake and regurgitated human beings. These birds usually brought men who killed, but Wolf of Shadows knew this one to be different.

He had heard its particular thrumming roar before. It would eject a certain human female, whose calm odor lingered yet in Wolf of Shadows' muzzle.

Last summer Wolf of Shadows had gone close to her, the only human being he had ever been near. She had not carried a death-stick. In her small odors was something that reminded him of the best smells of the forest.

She had stayed on the lake shore near where Wolf of Shadows drank. Day after day she had remained, until Wolf of Shadows grew used to her presence. Finally he showed himself to her, half curious, half challenging.

She had shared his gaze. Her eyes had grown wet as they regarded one another across a distance of three leaps. She had made an incomprehensible human growl: "Who are you?" Then she had fallen silent.

Their contact had made him watch her with wary interest. Her scent rose like the smell of the ground in the morning. Neither of them moved until a blackbird's fluttering passage had ended the moment.

Now her bird-thing swung and circled about, coming lower and getting louder. It roared and popped and sputtered. All at once it dropped in the lake, snarling and splashing. Then it was quiet. It smelled hot, sweet, tired. In the strange group of odors Wolf of Shadows also scented more creatures than the female. The human odors, distinct beneath those of the bird-thing, were as sour as the breath of terrified cubs. Wolf of Shadows felt the hairs along the back of his neck rise and tickle in the breeze. He growled, sniffing for some enemy.

The pack had awakened and withdrawn deep into the woods. For a long time the bird-thing remained motionless on the water. Fish began to splash again, and loons to call. Another odor added itself to the fear-scent: The flesh of one of the humans had been clawed by fire. At last the bird-thing began to regurgitate, expelling the humans from its craw. Their voices echoed across the water.

"I hurt, Momma."

"I know you do, darling."

"When is Daddy coming?"

"Soon, Carol. Come on, Sharon, let's get this raft inflated. And get our tent out of the cargo bay—hurry, honey."

The mother's voice was quick and breathy. Her shoulders were hunched as if against wind.

Wolf of Shadows responded to the suffering before him without thought, his ears back, his tail bowing. He whined. Hearing him, the littlest human cub babbled in terror. The mother's voice comforted, and her long forepaws held the burned creature close to her flesh.

"Momma, that's a wolf, isn't it?"

"You don't have to worry, kids, they won't hurt us. I know these wolves. I met one of them last summer when I did that research up here."

Behind the smells of tiredness and exhaustion Wolf of Shadows caught a whiff that made him recall their moment of contact last summer.

She and her healthy cub began to draw the burned one out of the bird-thing's craw. The injured creature's voice went shuddery. "Momma! You're hurting me!"

"Sharon, help me with her!"

"Momma, I'm doing my best!"

The burned cub's barks became ragged shrieks. From

21

her there poured a complex odor of roasted and dying flesh. Wolf of Shadows thought the cub might soon die.

They came closer, moving on the water. The three of them were jammed into a floating thing, bobbing across the lake. The healthy cub and the mother were paddling with their forepaws. The healthy one had soft fur on its otherwise naked human head. The other's fur was a crisp, stinking stubble. One of her eyes was swollen closed.

She made a noise: "I want Nana."

"She has to guard the house."

"Why? It burned. Everything burned. Oh, Momma, we're going to burn too!"

"We got out, darling. We're safe now."

The mother's growl was ragged. Her tone showed that she understood that her cub faced death. Wolf of Shadows wondered if she would make vigil when this happened. If she was like a wolf, she would mourn the death of her baby.

The three human beings went struggling up the bank, helping one another as best they could. From nearby Wolf of Shadows could smell their most intimate odors. The flatness of the burned cub's breath said that its life would soon depart.

The mother and the healthy cub carried bulky things in their forepaws, but Wolf of Shadows saw neither death-stick nor agony-jaws. They struggled with great flaps of skin until there was a den where there had been no den. Then they took the burned cub inside and began growling.

"Mother, I'm so sorry."

"Sharon—oh, honey, it's not your fault. She's a little girl, it was natural for her to be outside."

"The bomb was so far away. Why is she so burned?"

"Forty miles isn't too far for burns, not with a bomb that big."

"It was like a giant flashbulb, then she just—she was on fire."

There was a sound of bodies drawing close, and their odors grew warmer. "If you hadn't been on the porch . . . Oh, Sharon, I love you."

"I love you, Mother."

Their voices went on and on, deep into the night. Wolf of Shadows sat, not willing to go close to them, even less willing to abandon them. Every time he sniffed, the fire smell was stronger. The humans had deflected his attention, but he could not long delay his battle with the gray.

The mother's howl rose in the darkness.

"The river is wide, I can't get o'er, nor have I the wings to fly. . ."

She wailed with two voices. The one that could be heard was strong, for her cubs. The other, inner voice was full of fear. Then finally the wailing changed to a growl: ". . . through the valley of the shadow . . . the shadow of death . . . thy rod and thy staff . . ." It was a small sound against the dark.

The other wolves were indifferent to her suffering. During the first stirring of the birds they came close to the lake shore, skulking in tall grass where the human beings could not detect them. Wolves normally shunned man, but they had recently denned here and they were not eager to move their cubs.

As dawn broke, faint and hazy, the burned human cub began to scream, and this made the wolves creep away again, their tails down. The screams pitched back and forth across the lake, mixing with the morning chorus of the birds.

Wolf of Shadows trotted nervously out onto a spit of sand. His new position revealed an expanse of sky. The clouds smelled of char and smoke, not the freshness of fog and tang of lightning, which were the correct smells of clouds. And yet there was a certain wetness, a coolness that had not been there before. The fire-scent was strong enough now for any wolf to catch, but the pack was not interested in it because it smelled as if it had been doused by rain.

Wolf of Shadows did not lose interest in it. He inhaled, and smelled not cool but cold, and sensed a whispering ghost of snow.

A stronger smell came across to Wolf of Shadows: cold milk. Human voices rose again in complex growls.

"I can't find the matches, Momma."

"You said you had them."

"I dropped them, I must have! How could I be so stupid!" The healthy human cub rushed from the den moaning. When it saw Wolf of Shadows it stopped. He met its gaze, his body rippling with tension. All around it the other wolves hid, miserable and confused, wanting their denning ground back, but frightened of the humans.

"Mother! Look, Mother!"

The mother came out of the den. Her growl was smooth. "I know him. He's a very special wolf. Remember the pictures I took of him last summer?" She contacted him with her eyes. Hers was not quite a wolf's gaze, but neither was it the usual unsettling stare of the human being.

"Hello, black." Her call, so clearly directed toward him, made him cock his ears with careful interest. He lowered his tail. He wanted to run, but was unwilling to break contact. He growled.

She made a soft sound and held out her forepaws. The sound was not a growl, not a whine, certainly not a bark. It had the gentleness of the cub's whimper and the mother's squeak. Geese circled above, their honking flat in the silence.

Wolf of Shadows glanced up for only a moment. Then he returned his attention to the strange situation before him. He was interested in these humans. He remembered the meat the mother had given him last summer.

Then she broke the contact. Moving easily, the mother and the healthy cub returned to the den. There came an odor of meat, fatty but bloodless.

"Mother, I don't think I can eat this."

"That's perfectly good Canadian bacon, Sharon. You eat it now."

"It's raw."

"Sharon, it's precooked. You're just not used to eating it cold."

"I don't want it. Give mine to Carol."

"Eat it!"

"Okay, Mother."

"Carol honey, you try to eat something too."

The air was growing increasingly dank. The geese were now circling the lake, their voices raspy. Wolf of

Shadows had gone closer to the human den, drawn by the meat smell. In the entryway the mother clutched her cubs close to her. "Take it easy, black. Just take it easy."

There was a wariness in her tone that made him feel, suddenly, very alone. The pack wolves, still hiding in the grass, began to slink away. They were frightened by the least suggestion of human aggression.

Wolf of Shadows' loneliness rose in him. Something was being lost that he loved but did not even begin to understand. He threw back his head and howled.

The response shocked him into silence. The mother stood before her den, her legs apart, her head raised, her forepaws clutched across her breasts. She had howled back. "Well, wolf," came a choppy growl, "what do you think of that?"

"Mother, you shouldn't have done that. What if you make it mad or something?"

"Don't worry, Sharon. If I know anything, I know something about wolves. We were greeting each other—I think."

Her call had moved the other wolves to respond as well. In a moment the whole pack was replying, and the air was full of wolf voices.

"Mother, there are more wolves out there in that grass!"

"If they were hunting us they wouldn't be howling."

"But they might hunt us!"

"They won't."

"I hate this place!"

Inside the opening of the den the mother could be

seen touching her healthy cub with her mouth, then putting water on the raw flesh of the burned one. Strangely, she did not lick the wounds.

Wolf of Shadows whined. Death hung in the place, lurking in the rain and the stink of dead smoke. It lingered in the weakening breath of the cub, and in the miserable honks of the geese, which were landing.

The lead gander coasted down beside the bird-thing that had brought the people. Soon it was followed by another and another, and a great honking ensued. Wolf of Shadows was disturbed by its tone. Where was the joy of the geese, where was their contentious love now? The pairs went together, true, but they were not billing and rubbing as was usual in summer. Tufts of feathers fell from their wings when they flapped. Some of them seemed to be choking on their own craws.

One of them laid its head down on the water. Now it toppled to its side and, weakly flapping its skyward wing, began to go round in circles while its gander cried out.

Then the gander's head also sank, and then another. One by one they dipped their heads in the water, and flapped no more. They were blown about by curling breezes.

"Mother, look at those geese."

"They've been flying through a lot of fallout. We got out ahead of it. If it drifts up here at all, it'll be days. By then the worst of it will have faded."

"I'm scared. What's going to happen?"

"It's going to get very cold."

"It's June, Momma."

"It was a big war, Sharon. The clouds will block out the sun. June or not, we're facing winter."

"Why?"

"The soot stops the light—"

"I know about nuclear winter, Mother. We learned about it in science. But why was there a war? I didn't think there was even a crisis."

"Darling, we're not going to get any answers."

The growling went on, punctuated by sobs and protests from the cub. Wolf of Shadows had more important things to concern him than human noise. The breaths that he was taking in now were heavier and cooler than just a few moments ago. He sensed the nearby presence of a storm. A cool wind came down to the lake, ruffling the feathers of the dead geese, sending the bird-thing drifting toward the shore.

When Wolf of Shadows detected new human scents he pricked his ears to find the sound. The hunters from the other lake were approaching. Their voices were sharp and scared and their tramp was quick. Thunder rolled in the hills, and blue lightning momentarily brightened the pines. The wind whistled down from the sky and filled the air with the scent of a forest fire gone cold. Under that scent was the smell of melted flesh, lakes of it.

Wolf of Shadows flattened his ears to his head. The odors of summer were dissolving. The wind was like a claw, taking new shoots and grass tops, and spreading tender leaves among the dead geese on the lake.

Rain began, slipping as an owl slips from the sky, the big drops scattering dust where they fell, spreading perfect circles in the lake. Wolf of Shadows shook himself. The human mother and her cubs started growling again, and there were cries from the hunters.

As the storm shouldered its way across the hills enormous thunder slapped the water and bellowed in the pines. Lightning struck again and again, revealing the tossing trees and the shadowy bodies of the ruined geese, which blew aimlessly on the lake, collecting in a clump about the legs of the bird-thing. Through the cracks in the storm Wolf of Shadows heard the hunters coming closer and closer. He smelled their death-sticks and instinctively faded back into the protection of the trees.

The rain agitated Wolf of Shadows, for it was colder than it should be. It was also unlike any he had ever smelled before. It was full of fire-scent and the color of the lake shore mud. It came in driven drops, spattering the trees and the rocks, making everything gray.

The pack wolves drew their tails between their legs. The rain struck their backs, their flanks, making them drip with dark water. The air was gray, the trees were gray, the sky itself reached down and touched the lake.

The rain was so hard that it knocked the buds from the trees. Wolf of Shadows saw rivulets of gray run down the rocks, and saw the little den the human mother had made collapsed by the storm, and saw her struggling to hold it against the wild wind.

This rain made Wolf of Shadows long to seek the warm valleys beyond the range of the wolves. A sound like a bull moose blundering in the brush attracted his attention. It was no moose, though. The hunters had arrived. Wolf of Shadows moved farther back, watching them come around the lake. The hunters and the mother began growling at one another, their voices full of hisses and stifled snarls.

"Hey," a hunter cried.

"Hello!" The mother's growl was tight. "Have you got any medication—any antibiotics?"

"Nothing. Sorry. You up from Minneapolis?"

"No, from near Brainerd. I doubt if anybody made it out of Minneapolis." The mother sounded frightened enough to go for the hunter's throat.

He growled back. "What's going on? We heard something on the radio, they said there was an alert, then it went to static and all hell broke loose down south. We figure there's been a war."

She replied, her tone rising. There was no body language, though. Her ears remained steady, and she was without neck hair to raise. "There's been a war all right. An awful lot of places got hit."

"This damn storm part of it?"

"It's more than a storm. It's the beginning of a nuclear winter."

The hunters became still. Only their forepaws moved, inching slowly along the bodies of the death-sticks they carried.

"Meaning?" His tone told Wolf of Shadows that he was ready to spring.

"It's going to get colder, a lot colder. There's so much soot from the burning cities, the sun's being blotted out." Now the mother suddenly sounded as sad as a wolf who had just birthed a dead litter. "In a few weeks it'll be midwinter here."

The response of the hunter who had been talking was a mix of growl and yap. "Oh, Christ, we better go—where?"

"South, I guess, after the fires die down and the radiation subsides. We can use my plane. It seats six."

"What is that, a Cessna?"

"Yeah. I got it into the air just in time. We were lucky to live on a lake."

"Lucky, I'll say. That's sure as hell the only airplane around here."

"In a few days it'll be safe enough to travel if we don't fly over bomb sites."

"I might be able to fly a Cessna. I had some lessons back in the seventies."

"You can help me."

"But where the hell south should we go? If you're talking total war, you got no south to go to." There was so much whine in his tone that Wolf of Shadows thought surely he would roll and show her his belly.

The mother's voice grew soft. "There might be a corner somewhere, maybe along the Gulf Coast. We have to try." She might not lick her cubs, but her voice revealed a wolf mother's gentleness.

The growling among the humans went on and on, rising and falling in hypnotic waves.

Wolf of Shadows was feeling more and more strongly the need to lead the pack. His sense, if not his instinct, told him to expand the hunting range as in winter, not to stay close to summer's dens. He walked boldly up to the gray and touched his nervous muzzle, taking the scent of him.

He got a low snarl in response. The gray's shoulders were broad, his body long and firm, his claws and teeth unbroken. He was a healthy, strong wolf in his prime and he would put up a furious fight.

Wolf of Shadows snorted, shook his head, and snarled back—and was at once assailed by whipping wind and rain with black bits in it. The gray was afraid of the strange rain also, as were the humans who had gone back into their flapping den. The hunters could be seen when its sides blew open, eating the woman's fatty meat while she and her healthy cub sang.

"And when we find ourselves in the place just right,
It will be in the valley of love and delight."

If ever he had heard it, this was deathsong. The mother clutched her cubs beneath her, crouching in the den. The storm reached her anyway, and Wolf of Shadows could see in the dimness that water had made worms of her fur, and was running down her naked neck.

Then the mother stopped her singing and began to cradle the suddenly limp body of her burned cub.

"Carol, keep breathing! Somebody help us!" The older cub clapped her forepaws to her face. The hunters watched, chewing.

Suddenly the burned cub's scent changed; the warmth, the presence of breath, both disappeared. The flat, salty odor of dead blood replaced the living scents. All the wolves knew that the human cub had just died. Its mother knew, also. She began to whimper, rocking back and forth with the lifeless cub pressed against her chest.

The presence of death quickened instincts; the pack's mood changed. Always uneasy around human beings, they now wanted to get away from here. They had to run a short distance through the grass, then they could disappear into the woods. They hesitated, not wanting to show themselves even for the few instants necessary. Finally one of the young wolves made the dash.

Wolf of Shadows saw death-sticks start moving about in the hunters' arms. He wanted to attack them, but his memory of what they could do made him shrink away from their black mouths. Wolves leaped and ran as the death-sticks barked, their voices shattering even the sound of the storm. Wolf of Shadows ran with the others, his tail close against his haunches.

"Missed 'em!"

"Why do you have to kill everything you see?"

"Look, lady, those were wolves!"

"They're no danger to us, they're scared to death of us. Not only that, they're a rare species, they—"

"Lady, after what happened yesterday, I got a feeling we're rarer by far."

In the forest, Wolf of Shadows looked again at the gray. The time had come. The other wolf was stiff-legged, nervous. He wanted to drive Wolf of Shadows off, but he was afraid to try. The black wolf walked around the gray. This wolf was his brother, but to take the pack he was going to have to strike him hard.

The two wolves circled one another. The smell of fear in his rival's body-scent made Wolf of Shadows bare his teeth with slow menace, and then snarl. The gray tossed his head. He chose not to believe the challenge, and refused it by turning away. Wolf of Shadows would have none of that. He snapped. At last the gray's hair rose and he also bared his teeth.

Wolf of Shadows moved carefully. He blinked the rain out of his eyes, waiting for the moment when the gray's attention would wander. Around them the other wolves paused in their licking of one another and rose to their feet.

In a flash the gray came in, his muzzle twisting, his teeth touching Wolf of Shadows' throat. Wolf of Shadows leaped away, losing only some fur. He drew himself up and charged, putting his greater weight into the attack. The gray slipped, his claws rattling on the rocks. His eyes went so wide that Wolf of Shadows saw the whites. He pressed his advantage, going for the neck. He felt the matted, wet fur, tasted the flesh of his rival, then tasted his blood. Its odor swept through his muzzle, shocking him with its intensity. This was *wolf,* the very essence of the body, the hot life of it.

He bit to wound, not to kill. The gray reared back screaming, his eyes rolling. He took three long leaps away. Growling, crying, he shook his head while dark blood oozed out of his neck. Then he snarled as if ready to fight again. But he did not fight; his tail went between his legs. He turned away, trotted off a distance, then looked down. When Wolf of Shadows approached, he rolled.

Wolf of Shadows could not help it; he strutted. Then he nuzzled his brother wolf, feeling at the same time sorry for him, grateful to him, and full of love for the wolfness of him. The gray, who had taken them through many seasons, crouched beside him. They spent time licking one another's wounds, with the gray's mate looking warily on. Then they lay near one another in silence.

After a long time Wolf of Shadows directed his attention to the others. They were his pack now—if they would accept him. The females looked worried, the males hostile.

Tasting the blood in his mouth, the bits of fur still stuck in his teeth, he felt uneasy in his new position. He knew, though, that he was needed by these wolves. Only he had understood the danger of the storm, only he sensed the coming cold.

Wolf of Shadows threw back his head and howled. One by one the others joined him, until the pack had combined in a chorus of great complexity, expressing all the emotions of each of them. Even though the thunder muttered and the wind roared they heard the response of the other packs in the water country. After such a howl all the wolves within hearing would be excited, panting, filled with their feelings.

Only the gray's mate hung back. Her eyes were hooded, and when Wolf of Shadows went to take scent of her she lifted her lips, warning him away. He did not press himself on her. Rather, he honored her loyalty; she and the gray had been lifelong companions.

The power of his assault and the strength of his howl muted the rebellious feelings of the other wolves. Hesitantly at first, they began to come close to him. They moved carefully, each sniffing him, learning his tail-scent, looking at him and listening to him. He felt the pack bond as he had not since he was a cub, smelled it in their scents and heard it in the soft whuffling they made as they sniffed him. Two of the largest males submitted to him, rolling on their backs and baring throat and belly.

He had always wanted them, these with whom he had been born.

In the afternoon there was a brief time of thin light. From the lakeside there came the crunching of stone in wet earth as the humans made a hole. In it Wolf of Shadows could see the mother place the body of the dead cub. Then she whined over it. "Oh, God, take my daughter. God, preserve us, and give her a place within your love." Her voice rose a pitch. "God, please forgive us."

He separated her body-scent from the welter of smells in his muzzle and tested it. He could smell the prickle of fear, the thick salt of grief, the odors of her skin and her breath, and that calmness. Yes, sweet where most humans were sour.

She was not so disturbing to smell.

The remaining human cub began to whimper, rocking back and forth on its haunches, its long, wet fur waving as the willow waves. She and her mother embraced one another's shoulders with their narrow forelegs.

When darkness fell a night unlike any night that had been before came upon the water country. The air was filled with black, stinging rain, driven by a wind that wailed across the hills and made the lake foam. Lightning flashed and flashed, and in its glare the wolves witnessed a drama concerning the bird-thing that had brought the humans.

They had heard within the calls of the wind the strained murmuring of the hunters, who had denned near the mother and her cub. Their voices were crackling with fear.

Wolf of Shadows knew the violence of the hunters. He had seen them wearing wolf skin, and had seen the severed heads of wolves near their fire. Their den stank of burned blood and muscle, and over their territory marched the smoke spirit with its message of danger.

Moving stealthily, the hunters waded into the lake. Wolf of Shadows heard them approaching the great dark bird-thing, heard it open its craw for them with a scraping growl, then saw them entering it and the craw closing again. The mother and her cub did not notice this. But when the bird-thing began to cough and snarl they both jumped up, running to the shore of the lake, waving their forelegs and shouting.

Shafts of light pierced the gloom as the bird-thing awakened. The mother splashed into the lake, her paws raised in the lightning flashes, her voice pealing. The bird-thing's chattering rose to a whine and the creature swooped along the water. Soon its feet were slapping the edges of the waves. "You can't fly in this storm!" the mother screamed, her own body disappearing into the roiled lake. "You'll crash, damn you, you'll crash!"

The bird-thing rose into the clouds, its voice a buzzing shriek. It turned back and forth, the lights of its eyes darting crazily. As it went up its sound diminished. The mother stopped waist-deep in the water, then came back to shore, muttering, "Bastards, bastards."

Wolf of Shadows heard the bird-thing coughing and spitting far above. Then it gave a great whine. Again he saw its lights, now gyrating in the disturbed sky. The mother watched, and Wolf of Shadows smelled the dense sourness of despair in her scent.

The bird-thing, apparently maddened by the storm, came twisting and turning down and dived into the lake, raising a column of white foam. It did not come up again, and from the scent of the mother, Wolf of Shadows knew that the lake had claimed it.

The wolves huddled together, the females encircling the cubs, making little pools of warmth in the maelstrom. The males felt the wet edging beneath their fur, and shook their flanks to rid them of water and prevent their close hairs from getting uncomfortably damp.

The gray stayed a good distance away. All night Wolf of Shadows had heard the sound of him licking himself, and of his mate licking him. When their new leader looked their way, they averted their eyes.

Toward morning the storm stopped, and there was weak light. Wolf of Shadows moved from the other wolves, stepping carefully in the sticky mud. He sniffed the air. Where were the normal smells of the storm—the crisp odor of the washed air, the softness of rain puddles? The stink of spent fire covered everything. He moved from the forest where the wolves had hidden, loping down toward the lake. The water was turbid; the gritty rain had clouded it. There was no trace of the bird-thing that had drowned itself, or of the hunters who had been inside. The mother and her cub were hidden beneath the mound of their den. With the hunters gone, Wolf of Shadows found that he was not too uneasy here.

Even so, when the mound moved he stopped, instantly alert. Soon a long human paw appeared, and with a great cascade of murky water the mound opened. The humans stood up in a welter of their own body steam.

When they saw Wolf of Shadows the cub shrieked, a sound quickly stifled by the mother. "I told you, I know this wolf," she growled. Both of her paws came out, and Wolf of Shadows smelled the dirt on them.

She began to come closer to him. His short hairs rose, but he stood his ground. He watched her. Closer she came, and closer. He could see the light flickering in her eyes, could almost touch the tips of her outstretched paws with his nose.

She stopped. "Wolf?"

"Mother, look at its eyes, they're so strange."

The mother challenged Wolf of Shadows. He looked steadily into her dark pupils. Neither wolf nor woman wavered, nor wanted to. He inhaled deeply, trying to bring the sense of odor to his experience of her. The emotions in her eyes were at least as gentle as those in her scents.

Wolves bear as remembered smells the history of their lives, the kills, the hot summer nights, the odor of their winter coats, the drowsy, exciting mustiness of sex. Wolf eyes beckon and warn; they do not flicker with things beyond understanding, as her eyes did. She was so strange.

The wolf's experience of her gaze was interrupted by the faint vapor of acid rising from her belly. He realized that she was hungry—and so was he. As if by mutual consent, they broke contact.

His own hunger turned Wolf of Shadows' mind to

consideration of his new responsibility. The pack needed food to ward off the damp, and sustain them through the long journey ahead.

He trotted a short way toward the bald hill, intending to locate food and lead the pack to it. The two humans followed him, their paws slipping in the mud. He did not mind them. As they moved they made a snuffling noise, "Wolf, wolf, wolf." From them there came strong body-pungencies. During the night their pelts had thickened to puffy slabs of furless skin. Their paws were now also covered with extra skin, and new fur around their heads cast their faces in shadow.

When he began to lope they soon fell behind. He mounted the hill. On its far side was a valley where deer could often be found. Wolf of Shadows would take his pack to hunt for them. From the hilltop he looked out across the familiar view, and saw a fastness of gray shadows, black running clouds and mud. He inhaled. There was indeed an odor of deer, but very faint, stifled by the strong new smells.

The deer scent revealed that the animals were tired, meaning that they had been working hard. There was blood: one or more of them was injured, no doubt from struggling in the muck. They were frightened and alert, and would not be easy to catch.

He ran back down into the forest until he reached the pack. His appearance among them brought the other wolves to instant alertness. Ears pricked up, noses worked. They began to array themselves around him, eager for the hunt.

He trotted off a distance, signaling his pack that it

was to follow him. The cubs squalled protest when their mother uncurled herself and they felt the cold. Only one wolf, the gray, stayed behind. He stared sorrowfully down his muzzle, knocking his tail against the ground when Wolf of Shadows looked at him.

His mate came, her head held high, her eyes avoiding those of the leader.

In single file the pack climbed to the top of the bald hill. This was the first time since the storm that the other wolves had seen the wide landscape. As they sniffed the air and looked about them, one by one their tails went between their legs. Wolf of Shadows went on down the path toward the big valley below. They followed him. He began to move faster and still they followed him. He went on, loping into a long-distance gait, mud oozing up between his claws. Behind him came his wolves, their ears back, their eyes squinting against the rain, which was starting again.

They moved swiftly down the bald hill and onward through another patch of forest, crossing a good part of their broad range. Their pace quickened as they came out into the valley and caught sight of the deer, who were clustered in a ravine, sheltering from the wind.

Wolf of Shadows saw at once that this would be a difficult kill. The wolves had to trap the deer against the near wall of the ravine. But the mud made going hard, and it wasn't long before a white tail shone in the gloom and the rattle of little hooves sounded.

The wolves broke into a wild charge, their muscles straining to overtake the swift prey. Down into the ravine they went, following the bounding deer. The animals were so crazed with fright that they did not try to run up the ridge, but rather plunged into the mud on the windward side. Here their long legs and their hooves worked against them. Wolf of Shadows heard them whistling their gentle cries of terror as the wolves drew near. His blood raced in him, and the lure of their fear drew him on. Close beside him his wolves bore down on the slowest of them. He felt such joy that he snapped excitedly at the sullen air. He loved not only his wolves but the deer who gave the gift of the hunt, and were its reward.

Two of the young males were chasing a doe, and Wolf of Shadows went after the plunging, snorting buck. He nipped at its hindquarters and came away with a mouthful of fur, warm and full of deer scent. He whined, straining with effort, stretching, snapping the air. As the deer drew away, making a soaring plunge into a bank of wet mud, a gray shape appeared out of the gloom, moving in from the animal's flank. Wolf of Shadows recognized the gray's mate, and his heart soared up, that she was willing to hunt with him. She snarled, leaping just as the buck twisted. He was too late to avoid her, and she took him in the belly.

He screamed then, and faltered, and Wolf of Shadows mounted his back, closing his jaws around the bubbling throat, drinking in the salt blood of death as the deer collapsed.

Then he stood with this fine wolf, the gray's mate, panting with her over their steamy kill. They tore at the hot entrails, and the pack feasted. The kill was so rich that there was much meat left even when the wolves could eat no more.

After they had finished, the wolves drifted back across the land, the mother eager to regurgitate food to her waiting cubs. It was growing dark as Wolf of Shadows climbed his hill. The humans had watched the hunt from the hilltop, but when he came near they went back to their den by the lake. They huddled together, moving twigs rapidly in their paws and whining dismally. "It's just too wet. My hands'll be raw before I rub up a fire."

"I'm cold and hungry, Mother."

"Don't you think I am too!"

Long into the night Wolf of Shadows heard the low voices of the humans. From time to time fire winked and sputtered between their crouched bodies, but never for long. Toward dawn they hiked off toward the deer valley.

When they returned, they were carrying bones and bits of flesh from the wolves' kill. In the gray light of mid-day Wolf of Shadows watched them eat, blood running down their chins. They gagged and choked, sounding like displeased crows.

When he dozed Wolf of Shadows dreamed of the humans, their strange growling, their waving forelegs, and the mysteries in their eyes.

PART THREE

Black Ice

What is life? It is the flash of a firefly in the night. It is the breath of a buffalo in the winter time. It is the shadow which runs across the grass and loses itself in the sunset.

Last words of Crowfoot, 1899

Day AFTER DAY it rained. Soon the lake began to crawl up its banks, and the wolves were forced to move their cubs to higher ground. They huddled among the stones, their fur wet through, mewing and miserable. Wolf of Shadows remained certain of what he had to do: He must lead the pack on a journey, even beyond the farthest limits of their normal range, to find the sun.

He lay with the gray and the gray's mate. The gray was still nursing his wound, which had been healing slowly because of the wet. Wolf of Shadows was licking the gray's neck in the place where it oozed, when a new odor intruded. He stopped, raised his muzzle, sniffed carefully. When he understood what it was he jumped to his feet.

Into his face there fell not rain but sleet. Ice. The other wolves huddled more tightly together.

Wolf of Shadows shook himself, and then went off toward his hill, intending to see the extent of the sleet. On the way up his claws clattered on ice. When he reached the top a vicious wind struck him. The sleet stung his face, making him turn his flank to the storm's fury. In the distance below he could hear the humans groaning.

He loped back to the pack and roused them. Then he raced along the trail that led south, hoping that they would follow.

At first they just watched him. One or two of them trotted a short distance after him, then stopped. He rushed back, nipped a flank, danced around them, then bounded off again. After the first few paces he was running alone, the icy forest whispering past him.

He went back, looking for challenges. The gray cast his eyes down. A large wolf who had once or twice fought the gray snarled at Wolf of Shadows. Instantly they were fighting, Wolf of Shadows going for the throat, his adversary biting where he could. Then Wolf of Shadows clamped his teeth hard on the other's neck. He could taste his blood, could hear the air blowing in his windpipe. It was only a moment before the challenger's body relaxed. Wolf of Shadows released him.

The black wolf stood triumphant for a moment, then

turned and once again ran along the ice-crusted trail. Still his wolves hung back. He could break them all, one by one, but getting them to follow him was a matter not of strength but of loyalty, and that they had not yet fully given him. Even though time was short he had no choice but to wait.

Huddling with them through the long hours of the storm, Wolf of Shadows lost track of the divisions of the day. The sun and the stars became vague in memory. Reality was this ice.

The cold that was hard on the mature wolves was vicious to the cubs. Before the storms they had been growing well, rolling in the meadow, doddering about after beetles, playing at battle. Now they were nothing but bits of fur and staring eyes. The females kept close around them, but the wind and the ice seemed hungry for their lives. Day and night they mewed. When their mother licked them the spittle froze, making them look as if their little bodies had been wrapped by spiders. Their mouths hung open and their tongues became black and hard. Their eyes crusted, then closed. Sneezes shook them, and their heads bobbed when they stood. They never stopped shaking.

When the first of them died and the mother was deep in misery, Wolf of Shadows tried again to tempt the pack into the journey. They whimpered. The pack had always been in the water country. South where Wolf of Shadows wanted to go were the lands of man. The wolves wanted to be free in their own broad range, to run and run and never scent humanity.

There came a time, though, when days of hunting

were to no avail. They had to face the truth: The last deer had gone from the whole water country, killed and eaten, or wandered off.

Wolf of Shadows led a raid to the hunters' camp on the next lake, but it had been carefully stripped. He smelled the presence of the human mother and her cub, and saw where they had dug in the ice, also looking for food.

After their visit to the camp he had watched the humans make a small fire and burn roots in it. The two of them had leaped in the sleet and cried out joyfully when their flames rose.

As time wore on, hunger became the central fact of pack life. The two remaining cubs began to lose their hair from starvation. Their legs and necks got as thin as twigs. Wolf of Shadows was hungrier than he had ever been. *South,* the wind said, *south,* said the gnawing sleet.

One afternoon they took a starving opossum. When they were finished the humans came and eagerly gnawed the bones. Wolf of Shadows watched them at their feeding, breaking the bones with rocks and sucking out the marrow.

"Thank God they found something." The mother's growl was dull. She cradled her cub and made complicated little noises to her. "I love you, Sharon."

"I love you, Mother."

More days passed. The wolves trotted from lake to lake, crossed and recrossed the forest, went far up into the hills, but never caught a scent of game.

One day, as he had many times, Wolf of Shadows stood before the pack, then trotted away south. The wind was ruthless, racing through the icy forest like a living creature. He hurried along, not looking back.

Finally he stopped. Ahead was a frozen stream, and beyond it alien woods. He started across the twisted ice of the stream. Reaching the opposite bank, he turned. Far behind him stood the gray's mate. Without much hope he wagged his tail. The whole pack appeared, hanging just behind her. Then Wolf of Shadows saw one wolf moving past the others. The gray, his eyes glistening, his tail high, was coming to join him. His mate followed, and with her came the other wolves. Wolf of Shadows strutted. Then, head and tail erect, he set out into the frozen unknown.

The wolves did not set their usual traveling pace. Hunger had weakened them, they were too tired, and the cubs could not keep up. Night came, and they curled up among the trees. There was no sound but the wind and the endless, whispering sleet.

Then Wolf of Shadows cocked his ears. Far back on the trail he could hear a steady shuffling noise. The other wolves heard it too. Noses twitched, eyes stared into the gloom. Slowly the sound grew louder.

One or two of the wolves stood up, ready to fade back into the forest. Then a familiar sound filled the air—the growling of the human mother, followed by a whine from her cub. Soon Wolf of Shadows saw them, two lurching shapes making a huge din as their bulky skins scraped against the frozen brush that choked the trail.

Some distance away they paused. They had been moving fast, and their breath came in gasps.

"There they are, Momma."

"We've come miles. Just like I thought, they're going beyond their range. They're migrating, moving south."

"What about us?"

"Their instincts are telling them they can't survive up here. If they can't, we sure as hell can't either."

"You said radiation—"

"The worst of it will have dissipated. We'll have to take the risk."

"I'm tired. I don't want to walk."

"We're both suffering from malnutrition. We can scavenge their kills if they make any, and we're likely to come across canned goods."

"They're so fast."

"We can track them, dear. Not hard in this snow."

The wolves were soon on their feet again, moving through a night without moon or stars or end, keeping a sharp nose for prey. They blinked the ice from their eyes and breathed the fierce stink of the air. Thirst gnawed at them, for gritty snow and black ice were all they had to slake it. The ice was full of burned particles and tasted the way the air smelled. This scent was fire and more, hundreds of alien odors, none of them good.

If they did not find food soon, the mature wolves would face death along with the cubs. They went down through long valleys, toward the places where men lived. But there was no rising scent of humanity, no vast, earth-covering smell of man and thing. Instead there was only this ice.

Cattle and sheep and goats were no more, only lumps in the snow. They came to a human den that stank of fire and roasted bones, and sheltered against one of its walls.

They remained there for some time, sniffing curiously, trying to discover something more to eat than the blackened bones. Much later the tattered, panting humans appeared, the mother and her wheezing cub.

"A farm, Momma! Hello! Help!"

The cub was answered by the wind.

The two humans came loping up, the air whistling in and out of their noses.

"Sharon, stop! Don't go in there!"

"Momma—"

"Look at it. It's burned out. You might get hurt in there."

The cub clambered into a dark opening. There was a crunch of footsteps and the mother followed. "Sharon!"

The cub shrieked, bringing Wolf of Shadows to his feet. His hackles rose and he snarled.

"They're still in here, Momma. Oh, Momma, the whole house is full of burned people, and what's that—what's sticking in her chest?"

"It's an axe, Sharon. Don't look, honey."

The two humans clasped each other, and Wolf of Shadows sensed that the young one was suddenly less a cub.

"This was what I was afraid of. Looters. We stick as close to the wolves as we can now. They'll react if they smell other people."

"Why are they accepting us, Momma?"

"Sharon, I'm not sure I can answer that, but you can feel it, if you let yourself. We seem to belong with them."

Their earlier exploration had shown the wolves that there was nothing in the burned human den worth exploring. But night was beginning to fall. The bit of wall cut the wind, so the wolves remained curled up there.

"Look at them, they know what's best. We'll sleep now, too. Keep as close to them as they'll let us. Maybe one night they'll share their warmth with us."

When they came near the wolves, Wolf of Shadows laid his face on his paws and watched them. He was getting used to the way their odor mixed in with the rest of the pack.

Then they did the thing with their forepaws that made fire leap out onto some bits of wood. Wolf of Shadows watched, puzzled and nervous that they had let the fire out on the wood. No wolf moved, but every eye was on the dancing flames. They were ugly, but they were also warm, and the wolves did not move away.

In the late night the fire burned low. Wolf of Shadows stiffened but in the end did not resist when the human cub, shivering, nestled her paws beneath his body.

Morning revealed itself slowly. The congested shape of an apple tree frozen in bud emerged from the gloom. When Wolf of Shadows could see again he wasted no time; he struggled to his feet and shook. His spray of ice was swept away by the wind. Today they had to find food, or they risked becoming too weak to hunt.

They moved through a shadowy dream of the old human world. Thousands upon thousands of scents touched Wolf of Shadows' muzzle, none more distinct than the hazy air itself, and none trembling with the unmistakable vibration of a living body. Behind them came the two humans. Their voices rang in the wind, high with sorrow, as they moved from farm to town, past the dark openings of empty dens.

Shouting, they ran to a silent rolling thing, bigger than a bear, with huge round paws. In it sat dead men, their eyes closed, their faces frozen and gray. "You idiots, you left the engine on," the mother screamed.

"Momma, look in the back seat. There's all kinds of canned goods—look, beef stew!"

They became so excited that they made Wolf of Shadows put his ears back. He watched them warily as they swarmed over the thing, taking little round objects that smelled cold and dropping them into pouches in their furless pelts. Then they released fire. They manipulated the round objects and set them beside the flames. The wind made the fire writhe, and soon a powerful odor of burned flesh came up.

The wolves watched the humans eat, and then Wolf of Shadows went and put his tongue in one of the shells that had contained the food. The taste was sharper than blood, not unlike that of little creatures left in the wake of a brushfire. His belly seemed to twist on itself, he was so hungry. He salivated, and his drool froze on his jowls.

"You poor things," the mother growled. Then she opened another of the shells and a powerful odor of salt came out. "Salisbury steak," she said. Wolf of Shadows ate it in a single gulp. Behind him his pack stood, hesitant, fascinated by the food odors, uneasy at being so close to the humans. The mother growled. "We've only got four more cans."

Then the wolves had food, and in a moment it was

gone. So little! A small female, who had gotten nothing, whined miserably. The mother began regurgitating for her cubs, and the little creatures' eager licking was for Wolf of Shadows a better song than the highest, deepest howl.

Smelling nothing more to eat, Wolf of Shadows led his pack off through the tumbled maze of the human place. Beyond the dens there were long lines of the round-pawed things, and frozen humans sitting in all of them. The lines stretched away over the rolling hills, on and on. The frozen human beings sat with their eyes open or closed, their faces in peace or agony, their hands around their bodies or clutching parts of the things they were in.

"My God, it's a traffic jam of the dead. Oh my God."

"Mother, why are they all dead?"

"This many cars—they probably started out from the Minneapolis suburbs. They must have died of radiation poisoning, or maybe there was some kind of gas—I just don't know."

"Momma—" The two humans clutched each other so tightly that they seemed for a moment to be a single creature. "Momma, let's stay here. We can eat canned food and live—live in a car or something."

"It's getting colder by the hour. Sooner or later it'll get too cold for us to survive."

"Mother, we're used to cold. It was thirty below last January and we were out in it."

"A hundred below would freeze your lungs. And it might get colder than that. I don't know."

The young human made a coughing sound and dragged her forepaws through her fur. The mother comforted her, rearranged the young creature's hood, and made more sounds. "We have to keep moving. The farther south we go, the more of a chance we have."

The long lines of frozen things were silent, glistening with ice the color of a weasel's eye.

Wolf of Shadows loped on. He traveled until his paws smarted and his breath made a cold place in the center of his chest. Nowhere did he smell living flesh. They had been moving along beside the line of dead things for most of the day, and still it had not ended. From horizon to horizon stretched the disorderly row. Far back the two humans were tiny, moving dots beside it. As night came on, the wolves stopped. Much later the humans caught up. "They're here, Mother."

"Were lucky they're moving slow."

"Look at them, they look dead. They must be exhausted."

Soon the humans began to make breaking sounds, and then they entered one of the frozen things. Wolf of Shadows could see them inside struggling to throw out its rigid occupants. As they worked, the smell of their skin grew sharper. Their breathing was harsh against the wind.

"It won't start, will it, Mother?"

"Not with a frozen battery, but it'll be shelter from the wind."

Far off—from across the horizon—Wolf of Shadows suddenly scented something of intense interest. He cocked his ears, but the smell was from too far away to be accompanied by sound. It was an odor of human flesh, alive. For a moment it lingered in Wolf of Shadows' muzzle, then it was taken by the wind. He would not lead his pack in the direction of that scent. The mother and her cub were familiar; strange human beings meant danger.

The night passed, and another day, and then another night. When the humans continued to give the wolves food from the shells, the wolves began to take more interest in them. They no longer moved quite as fast as they had before, and they slowed down when the humans were far behind. When the pack heard the hiss of the food shells opening they would go to the humans and wait just out of reach of their long, naked paws.

Daily the cold deepened, and the pack kept moving, the wolves trotting, the humans trailing along behind. As they went south they also found a few prey animals. One day they killed a deer. Another they came across some dogs and killed them. The signs of man were all around them, but man himself was nothing but that one trace they had smelled.

One of the two surviving cubs began to make rattling sounds in its throat. It shook, its eyes pleaded, and its mother sniffed it sadly. The gray's mate licked it as best she could in the cold. She kept its dribbling nose clean, and when they rested she let it burrow under her neck.

One evening the human mother came near the cub and the gray's mate, and the wolves growled. They had come to tolerate the food-giving humans, but not near the cubs. The human mother was persistent though. She squatted with her paws out. There was meat in her paws, and the gray's mate smelled the meat. Wolf of Shadows would have taken it at once, but the female was very careful. Finally she reached out her graceful muzzle and took the chunks of bland food. She regurgitated for the cub, and the human mother moved closer.

A change in the female wolves' scent told Wolf of Shadows that they were going to tolerate the human. That night the cub sheltered with the humans in the back of one of the frozen things. At last it was truly warm. The next day it walked again, and soon was traveling with the other cub. The gray's mate, the cub's mother, and then the other wolves ceased to be wary around the two humans, and Wolf of Shadows began to like the way the pack smelled when they were in it.

Often Wolf of Shadows listened to the growling of the humans, alert to know whether or not it meant food. It was fascinating in its complexity even though it made little sense.

"Maybe we'd be better off finding a few other people."

"You saw what happened at that farmhouse. You want to risk that? We're safer with wolves than men."

"We can get a gun."

"Somebody already looted every car we've opened for guns. Think about it. Do you want to meet that somebody out here all alone?"

The low growling stopped. For a moment the two humans glared at one another like angry wolves. Then the growling resumed, and grew louder. A cry snapped through the snowy air. The human mother had struck her cub. "You *will* keep going, by God you will!" And then the long cough of tired lungs, and their voices dissolving into silence.

Suddenly the two of them threw their forelegs around

one another. Wolf of Shadows saw how thin their bodies were as their pelts flapped about. He went closer to them and would have licked them to comfort them, but neither presented for it.

That night the wolves curled together in some shrubs. By dawn the air had changed, becoming to sensitive muzzles like the needles of the porcupine. Morning brought no fresh scents and more disappointment: The cub that had gotten well had sickened again, and been taken as suddenly as a leaf on the wind. Its little body lay in the snow, a tuft of fur, no more. The one remaining cub whined, his voice sounding very alone.

The scent of the air was terrifyingly simple: There was nothing left alive in this land but the wolf pack and the two human beings. The mother groaned as the wolves trotted off. "I'm sorry they lost that cub. I just wish I'd been able to save it."

On this day they began to pass through the edge of a very strange place. Here the air was filled with upsetting odors, the smell of fire and acid smells and flat smells and sharp ones, the smell of rotted flesh and that of burned flesh, of seared hair and wood, of burned men and animals.

On one side of the place rose low hills covered with ice and ruins. On the other, stretching to the end of eyesight, stood a vast, tumbling forest of caved-in, burned human dens. Ice had covered it over and the ruins were hazy beneath its gleaming surface. The heavy ice made sounds, like the crack and groan of the lake in winter. Wind howled past its corners and overhangs, and boomed in its depths.

Coming from the ruins there was another sound—the drip of water. The wolves had been eating snow and licking ice for days. Now, suddenly, there was amid this desolation the scent of free running water.

Wolf of Shadows headed toward the smell. It was far into the ruins, in a place where a thick-scented vapor rose from the ground. He began to trot toward the spot, taking care not to cut his paws on the twisted jumble just beneath the ice. The humans, still some distance behind the wolves, began suddenly to run after them.

"No, no, don't go that way! Hey, heyaah! *Heyaah!*" The sticklike human mother ran up, her cub not far behind. Wolf of Shadows felt threatened by the violence of her motions. He put back his ears. "Downtown Minneapolis is that way. Get back, get back!"

"Momma, this can't be Minneapolis, where's the—"

"Help me turn them, honey. They're going right toward ground zero!"

The mother's bellows slammed into the wolves' ears and made them shake their heads. When she got between them and the water, they gave up and slunk away on their bellies—all but Wolf of Shadows, who would not let her overcome him. He stood glaring straight at her eyes. She stared back, and did not avert her gaze. His body felt the threat and he growled. She growled back, "I can't let you do it."

He did not know quite how to react. Nervously, he growled again. She strode toward him, her forepaws coming together and making loud sounds like limbs snapping. When he tried to circle her she came rushing over and grabbed him. A shock coursed through his body. He writhed away from her, his every impulse to snap hard.

Their eyes met again, and he saw softness. Then one of her paws caressed his ear, and a thrill of pleasure went through him.

Her throat was working with little sounds. He found that he liked her to put her paw against his ear. He let her caress him, and was glad inside. But then her other long foreleg came around his neck, and for an instant she confined him. A shock of revulsion shattered the pleasure he had felt. He shook his head, and moved away from her.

The water forgotten, he caught up with the pack.

The condition of this place was a mystery to Wolf of Shadows. It had been an enormous human territory of the kind he had smelled when he had come down from the water country long ago. Now these gaping ruins stretched from horizon to horizon, broken by long, flat paths choked with dark lumps of ice. The wolves walked down one of the paths at the edge of the ruins. Along a nearby wall, still standing to their full height, were black shadows of men. Their bodies were gone. But these shadows remained, some with forelegs raised over their heads, some at full run, some shielding the shapes of cubs. The shadows were as clear as if they had been cast by the full blaze of the sun.

A running multitude had left their shapes here. Where had they gone? Wolf cubs often tried to run away from their own shadows, but they never succeeded. Humans were mysterious.

The black wolf touched a lump of char with his nose and smelled bone. He sneezed, not expecting the smell of a burned animal. But then he noticed something that made his attention as sharp as a claw. He was standing on a crust of ice, and beneath this crust was more of the same char, much more. The expanse between the ruins was not land at all, but a mound made of vast quantities of burned humans. Beneath the ice Wolf of Shadows could see skulls and teeth and scorched bones. He turned and ran away from the place of death, and his pack followed him.

When at last the awful smell had dwindled enough for him to slow down he felt the wolf mother brushing against his flank and moaning. She had the last cub in her mouth. She dropped it at his feet.

He looked down at the tragedy before him, a miserable hank of wet skin, its fur almost gone, its eyes closed, its tail curled stiff. He could not meet the eyes of the mother, and he was meek as she took his neck in her jaws and shook gently.

The young of the season were lost, but the living had to go on. He resumed following the edge of the ruins.

From far away the wolves heard a sound that made them inhale deeply, scenting for danger. It was the bark of a death-stick, then of another and another. There was man-scent, very faint, and then the scent of warm blood.

The human mother and her cub gave no sign of knowing that others of their kind were nearby. Often they missed even important noises.

The wolves soon began to pass an immense den set amid a horde of rolling things, all of them burned. The den was a tangle of giant, fire-blackened limbs, like a huge old oak burned in the woods. From it there arose the scent of an immense quantity of burned, frozen human flesh. In the gloom Wolf of Shadows could see a charred multitude.

To put living sound back in the world the wolves howled. The humans answered with a long, high sound of their own. Wolf and human they might be, but their voices joined were more than each alone. For a time the howls traded back and forth, but not for long because none wished to linger in that place. Wolf of Shadows marked a steady pace south, always keeping to the edge of the icy ruins. Hour after hour they trotted along, and still the ruins remained beside them.

Then he noticed a new odor, one that he did not like. It was the blade-thin sourness of fresh canine scent-marks. They got fresher as the pack moved. Ahead was dog country. Wolf of Shadows murmured deep in his throat, then stopped and lifted his leg, covering one of the foul little marks with his own rich urine, smothering it in a good aroma.

He drew air deep into his nose, feeling its coldness far up his muzzle. Sure enough, he detected behind the odor of their marks the smell of the dogs themselves. The age of the scent told him that they were within a few hours' trot. It also said that there were many of them, some sick or injured, others healthy. He smelled as well that they had made a fresh kill.

The pack moved steadily on, through an ever more ravaged landscape. There were no more tumbled ruins here, but rather the fallen bones of trees, and the scattered shambles of human dens. Everything had been shattered and cast down, and now lay under the ice in blackened piles.

As they moved, the dog-scent became stronger and

they trotted faster. The wolves would take their kill from them, whatever it was. Wolf of Shadows could feel the excitement of the others. The young wolves came close to him, temporarily displacing the gray's mate, who had taken second place in line. The gray himself was far back, still suffering with his old wound.

The wolves spread out across the landscape in a broad row. They continued for a time like this, until Wolf of Shadows saw the first of the dogs. It was a bedraggled creature, its coat matted, its tongue lolling. It stood on a low rise, panting.

The smell of the dogs' kill grew stronger. Wolf of Shadows' skin grew taut and his body quivered. He could feel his other wolves around him, and was glad for their kinship. His wandering past seemed very far away.

A dog gave voice, but not in alarm. As they got closer and closer yet, the wolves heard the dogs snarling among themselves. The one on the rise finally detected them and began to bark. None of the wolves made a sound.

The first of the dogs turned and sought its pack when the wolves came too close to it. A great commotion of barking ensued.

The wolves moved on, silent.

The barking grew more strident. Wolf of Shadows heard it change from anger to rage, then to fear. As the wolves got closer, they saw the reason for the dogs' fear. To escape the wind they had backed up against a wall. The wide hunting approach of the wolves prevented the dogs from leaving; their shelter had become a trap.

They were as miserable a lot of creatures as Wolf of Shadows had ever seen. There was one enormous thing that looked like a possible threat. Its hair shone with black ice, its teeth gleamed, and one of its ears was scabbed over from a savage tear. Clearly it was pack leader. In addition to it there were a number of dogs with faintly wolflike looks, and one quite beautiful bitch with a fine, proud tail. In this bitch's mouth was something that made the wolves put their ears back. The dogs had turned on their human masters.

The wolves were famished. They would be indifferent to the carrion, though, as long as there was a chance at the flesh of the dogs.

They went in fast, on their bellies, moving for a kill rather than the dominance fight the dogs expected. They were not interested in the hierarchy of these creatures. Dogs were meat.

Wolf of Shadows singled out a medium-sized dog with a look of exhaustion about it. This one had dragged the haunch of their kill and was tired. Wolf of Shadows went straight for its throat, while the other wolves snapped at the rest of the dog pack. The creature growled and bit, drawing its head down and trying to present its attacker with a row of teeth instead of a soft neck. But Wolf of Shadows was quick, much quicker than a dog. He felt the icy fur in his mouth, then the skin and the salty leather band around the creature's neck. Instantly he snapped, then twisted its head. The dog screamed, its neck spurting blood. It tried to bite the wolf but missed, then fell back, rolling in its death agony. The shiny things attached to its leather band jingled as it quivered its last. It wasn't much, but it would fill some bellies.

The other dogs now attacked the wolves in a wild and

desperate melee. Fangs shone in the half-light and voices were raised to screaming. Again and again Wolf of Shadows felt the searing rip of a wound. Little dogs, big dogs, dozens of them, were swarming into the fight.

Being trapped had crazed them. They were weak but they were also many. As hungry as they were, the wolves had to run even though fresh kills lay on the ground before them. The young females were the first to break. Behind them came the rest of the pack, holding off the torrent of dogs, and then Wolf of Shadows and the gray's mate, fighting side by side as if they were old partners.

When they had finally all broken off, the pack paused to lick its wounds, and when the gray's mate licked Wolf of Shadows his heart filled with gratitude.

After the wolves left, the dogs could be heard fighting frantically among themselves for the remains of their own dead.

The wolves trotted on, far into the night. The wind howled and the ice fell in waves. Soon they were passing through rolling country. Here the dens of men still stood, but they saw no lights and smelled no smell of life.

Much later Wolf of Shadows heard the humans, and at last they appeared, struggling to raise their hind legs from the ground. They stumbled into a half-collapsed den and the wolves came near, their noses twitching expectantly. Would they find the food hidden in the shells, the food that had no scent until they touched it?

There came from the den a howl of rage. "They took everything. There isn't even any garbage!"

"Calm down, Mother."

"Sharon, I didn't know I could be this hungry!"

The sadness and anger in these sounds made the wolves whine. They were not the sounds the humans made when they found food, and the wolves were again growing desperate. A few of them were shaking all the time, and when the pack stopped most had to lick sores on their paws. Their ribs showed.

When later Wolf of Shadows drew into his nose a marvelous, familiar, and forbidden scent, he quivered with delight. It was the odor of a fat, slow cow, the kind men kept behind fences and guarded with death-sticks. A wolf would normally avoid a cow even though its meat was richer than that of a moose, because cows were always close to men.

But the rules had changed. Taking this cow would mean life. The creature's odor had risen in warm fur, and was mixed with that of warm, dead grass. Not only did the cow-odor attract the wolves, so did the warmth.

Wolf of Shadows estimated the creature to be a trot to the south, but not so far that his wolves couldn't make it. They went off eagerly, their tongues lolling, their bellies growling. They could not help leaving the humans far behind.

As they trotted along, sustained by the delicious scent, they heard familiar cries up in the wind: Geese and ducks were abroad in the sky. South of the great ruin some birds still lived. In all their many languages only two things were being spoken: We are cold; we are lost.

The land, though, was quiet. Where beaver once had cut the underbrush there were no living things. No paddle tails slapped the frozen water when the wolves passed;

raccoons did not scream nor opossums faint.

As they came closer to the scent of the living cow, other scents rose, death-scents and something wonderful, rich and delicious: milk. The wolves whined and raised their muzzles to it, drooling helplessly. But Wolf of Shadows gave warning: They had to be careful, because man-scent was there too, even though it was steeped in fresh blood.

When they were so close they could see the large, dark den where the animal was kept, they stopped. A short distance away the smaller man den flickered with light. There were no voices, no sounds of movement. The smells of death and blood came from the human den, and the smell of the milk. There was warmth lingering in the milk scent, it was so fresh.

In its own shelter the cow began to blow and stomp its hooves. It smelled the wolves.

Wolf of Shadows sat down. The others followed his lead. They would not act until the light in the man den went out or continued silence convinced them that the men really were dead. Hunger gnawed; the wind blew through their summer coats. One or two of them whined softly, shifting on their haunches. The ashen, frozen air had been hurting their muzzles. Even Wolf of Shadows had noticed a disturbing reduction in his sense of smell. They had been almost within sight of this place when it began to reveal its small odors. Once he would have smelled them from a long trot away. Had the cow-scent been light, they would have missed the kill altogether.

Presently there came a familiar sound from behind

them, the shambling, clattering, muttering arrival of the human mother and her cub. The wolves cocked their ears, and a tail or two gave a wag. Only with their arrival did Wolf of Shadows feel that the pack was complete. Their scent had become part of its order.

"Lights, Momma! They've led us to a lighted farmhouse!"

"Oh, wolves, thank you." They ran to the man den and began pounding at the door with their long, supple forelegs. Slowly it creaked open.

A sharp shriek pierced the air.

"It's milk, Mother, all over the floor!"

"Careful, honey."

"Mother, what happened here?"

"I think there was a fight."

"Over the milk?"

"Over the milk."

"They're all cut up."

The moaning growls went on for a long time. Wolf of Shadows whined high in his throat to remind the two creatures that he was with them, he and his wolves.

"There's no food, there was just this milk. About two quarts, I'd say. And I could scream, because it's *spilled!*"

"Be glad the house is still standing, Mother. If we're going to stay here we've gotta get rid of the corpses. Get 'em out in the cold."

"For the wolves to scavenge? I couldn't bear to see that."

"Mother, they're going outside."

"I can't put them out, Sharon, not and see them eaten."

A growl, angry. "There's kerosene. We'll wrap them in some sheets and burn them."

When the door of the human den opened, Wolf of Shadows came to his feet. He felt more comfortable now that the mother and the cub had revealed that the human den held no surprises.

After a moment they came backing out, dragging between them the body of a human male. It had a silver stick coming out of its chest, and a gash had almost severed its head from its neck. They laid it on the ground and then brought another. This one's head was shattered.

Then came three thin children, all with vines grown tight around their necks, and a woman, her throat slit, and a man, his face covered with the marks of many blows, his forepaws clutching a nasty silver claw full of blood. He had fought hard, this man. Wolf of Shadows smelled the blood of the two dead men on the silver thing, and on a blunt iron hook the human females threw near the corpses.

Wolf of Shadows was confused to see them pour foul-smelling liquid over the dead humans. Then fire came up from the bodies, and the human females growled. "God rest them and keep them."

Soon they sealed up the den and Wolf of Shadows could no longer read the emotional sense of their growls. He was learning some of their language, though. He knew the growls that meant hunger and exhaustion, the growl of victory over prey and the one for pain. He also knew the low sounds they made for love, and the gulping moans of their sorrow. They never moved their ears, and their hair never rose. They had no tails to express fear or joy, or to lend shades of meaning to their growls and howls and barks. Their place in the pack was at the rear, and given their missing parts, that was as it should be.

The wolves soon forgot the burning bodies and turned their attention to the more tempting prey: the cow. They moved quickly around the animal's den, sniffing the base of the wall for a telltale strengthening of the odors within. This would indicate a weak spot in the wood. A crack could be made larger. Soon Wolf of Shadows found a likely place. The other wolves began digging with him. Inside the shelter the huge bovine began to bellow. The odor of its spittle mingled with the penetrating smell of urine. The animal was terrified.

A sudden shaft of light fell across the barnyard. The mother's silhouette appeared in the door of the human den. A glowing eye was attached to her forepaw. It raised itself into the dark. The woman cried out, "A cow, Sharon, a cow in the barn! That's where the milk came from."

Wolf of Shadows watched the sleet falling through the strong beam of the light, and wondered why humans let themselves be dragged around by things.

The light pulled the mother closer to the bovine's shelter. "Hey, cow," she whined. "You beautiful thing, are you okay?"

There was now no sound inside the cow den, but the human mother did not react even to the overpowering aroma of the cow's terror. The light kept her in the doorway while it cast itself about, resting first on a frozen chicken, then on the door of the cow's den.

"Cow?"

The light drew the mother even farther from the human den. Behind her came the young female, who had

72

until so recently been a cub. There was still cub-scent about it, though, and Wolf of Shadows thought the mother ought to have kept it away from the hunt. He thought about punishing her with a nip. She should be able to control her own issue. It was, after all, the youngest creature left in the pack.

He crouched as the mother came nearer. He would give her a lesson. The mother's lips were dry and cracked and her breath smelled acid with hunger. Wolf of Shadows looked at the veins pulsing in her scrawny throat. She would be glad of the food tonight, poor creature. Just when he was about to challenge her, she turned away, no doubt sensing his anger.

"Cow? Are you all right? I won't let those wolves in there, you don't have to worry about that." Wolf of Shadows read fear in her whines. Good, she had gotten his message without the need for a nip. In a moment she would be going back with the young female.

Her forepaws rattled the hard vines on a wall of the cow's den. "Locked. It's just as well, but now we can't get in any more than the wolves can."

"We've got to find the key."

"Sharon, it would have been in somebody's pocket."

The young female sighed. "I'll poke around in the ashes for it." She went back to where they had burned the bodies from the house. Making little cries under her breath, she moved about, staring at the smoking rubble. Then she reached down and picked up something from the pile of burned flesh. It jingled, this little thing.

She put it into contact with the vines, and then Wolf of Shadows saw a miracle. The wall became an opening.

The light went into the den, dragging the humans behind it. "You settle now, cow. Nobody's coming in here but us." There was relief in the mother's voice—and no wonder, since the den's opening meant the pack would not have to dig under its walls, and there would be meat all the sooner.

Then the light upset everything. The nasty little thing turned around and took the humans outside. Next thing Wolf of Shadows knew, the jingler had closed the den again and that was that. The two humans went trotting back to their own shelter.

Anger made the wolves dig with furious energy. As they worked they grew more heated and more eager. The cow had begun stomping again. They could hear it pulling and pushing and jumping in its confined space. Wolf of Shadows dug until his paws stung, and the sensitive skin at the base of his claws was raw and tender. He was so hungry he bit the ground. The others, digging beside him, worked just as hard. All their bellies were tight knots of pain. As he dug, Wolf of Shadows could almost taste the rich meat that was so close. He plunged his burning paws into the earth, and eagerly snapped again at the soil.

Memories of other kills filled his mind—of old moose welcoming death with dignity, of deer who would not go down, of fat mice, of raccoon and opossum. He imagined himself gobbling his fill.

Suddenly the fantasies were replaced by a beautiful reality. Rich, warm, cow-thick air! Another moment and they would be through.

The humans came out of the man den growling their eagerness. "Cow, what's the matter?"

Wolf of Shadows barely flicked his ears in their direction. Unless they helped in the kill, they had to wait. If they came much closer, the wolves would show them teeth. They did not belong so much to the pack that they could demand a place without joining the kill.

"Wolves, no!" Ears went back. "Momma, they're digging a hole." Another step and the humans would be reminded of their place. "You can't get in there, can you, wolves?"

"I don't think they can, Sharon. Look, wolves, here are chickens. We'll thaw them out for you. You can eat carrion, you lucky creatures."

There was a frozen bird in her forepaws. She dropped it to the ground. Compared to the cow, it was of little interest.

"They're really hungry, Mother."

"I know. We've got to get them fed, I think, or they'll knock themselves out trying to get that cow, which they must not do, not if we're going to use her for milk."

"They're digging again, Momma. They'll tear their paws to shreds." The young female's voice was steady, a tightness in the tone.

The human mother growled. "The poor things are starving. They want that cow. Come on, let's get a fire going. When these chickens are thawed they'll smell strong enough to deflect their attention. Otherwise they'll wear themselves out trying to dig through the frost." She disappeared into the man den.

Beneath the hard surface the dirt was soft and faintly warm from the matted hay on the other side of the wall. Wolf of Shadows was soon through the hole, jamming his head into the opening, dragging himself forward with his paws, until at last he was in the shelter. It was so full of cow-scent that at first his stuffy muzzle could not locate the creature.

Then he heard it breathing and saw its great hooves just showing beneath a length of board. In one long leap he was standing atop the cow's stall. The other wolves were coming into the shelter one by one, shaking dirt from their flanks. The cow's eyes rolled. It was too young to want death, despite the fact that it was not strong.

The cow kicked the boards that confined it, raised its snout and bellowed. Wolf of Shadows leaped on the cow's back and at once began probing with his long muzzle for the soft flesh where the lifeblood ran. He snapped but could not reach it, not without getting down where the hooves were pounding. If he was very careful, he might be able to turn around, slip under the cow's middle, and open its entrails. But then how did he prevent the creature from collapsing on him and suffocating him?

The gray's mate came up beside him, worrying the cow's snout to make it lift its head. Wolf of Shadows jammed his muzzle down toward the throat while the female pulled back the nose, and the creature's bellows became husky gasps. He felt soft skin, and within it the end of his tongue could detect a huge, throbbing vein. His teeth first touched it, then gripped tight. With a toss of his head he cut it completely in two. Blood poured from the wound, hissing into the hot hay.

The cow's voice died to low moos, then a series of choked bleats. It shook its head as Wolf of Shadows gobbled bite after bite of its flesh. The others were all on it now, swarming over its back, gnawing and tearing and choking down huge mouthfuls of the rich meat. The creature went to its knees, then to the ground. A cry came from beneath it, one of the younger males. As the cow collapsed the cry went high and thin and then was stifled.

There was little mourning. That wolf had died a foolish death.

Wolf of Shadows was so absorbed in his eating that he did not at first notice the screams echoing up and down the barn. Then the sounds penetrated his pleasure, and he raised his head. The human mother was not two feet away from him, her forepaws raised, her eyes bulging.

He saw a silver claw in her paw, the one that had been in the hand of the dead man, and had the blood of the dead on it. He saw it rise up, her foreleg swinging down from it like a vine from a branch. If he did not jump away the claw was going to slash his shoulder. He dodged aside, his eyes never leaving those of the challenger.

He cowered back—but there was a wall behind him. The other wolves were slinking off into the shadows, their muzzles smeared with meat and blood.

He had only seconds. He could do but one thing— leap at her and teach her the lesson she needed to learn. He did not want to do it to her. But the silver claw now ruled her movements. He jumped even as a searing blow crossed his back. When he opened his jaws to take the throat of his enemy her eyes broke the challenge.

With a snarling cry she threw down the claw and dropped at his feet. He could not avoid shouldering her as she fell. She was slammed aside and her head thudded against the boards that had confined the cow. Moaning, she lay as a cub might lie, curled up in the hay. When he looked upon the sadness in her face, Wolf of Shadows whimpered and nuzzled her.

She lay helpless beneath him, groaning and sputtering as he licked her, smearing the blood of the cow on her furless skin. Her throat was pale in the dark. When he cocked his ears he could hear the blood hissing in her veins. His own wounded back did not concern him; the claw had merely scratched the skin. When the blood stopped, so would the pain.

The mother's eyes opened, slowly refocused, and once again met the wolf's. She growled softly, and Wolf of Shadows responded to the tones, which were very strong, of sorrow and of loyalty. A shiver of joy went through him. Now that he had vanquished her rebelliousness, she would truly belong to the pack. He bent his head and licked her side where he had hit her, as he would the wounds of a fellow wolf.

She lay before him, showing her belly.

Wolf of Shadows howled. His feelings had overwhelmed him, just as they did on spring nights when the air was filled with humid love, or in autumn when the dark brought a new sharpness to the eyes in the sky, and the death of the land filled a wolf with longing.

When some of the younger wolves, less sensitive to the rights of the followers than he, tried to express dominance over her, he warned them away. She had already been shown her place.

After eating they stretched out and began to sleep in a pile on the floor. As soon as all was quiet, the human mother rose up and rushed from the barn, her voice high and frantic. Many times in the night Wolf of Shadows heard her wailing with the young female. "What else can we do? We'll keep on following them."

"We can get south on our own, Mother."

"And blunder into God knows who. They'll guide us, Sharon, away from people and toward food."

"They're all sneezing a lot. Do you suppose they still have a sense of smell?"

"Maybe not as good as it was, but better than what we have—our ears can't really hear, our eyes overlook important details, our noses tell us nothing. We need their senses to survive."

Wolf of Shadows slept fitfully, dreaming of the human mother's eyes and her flashing claw, and wet, hot blood.

He awoke suddenly.

What was this? No more sound of wind. No more sleet hissing against the shelter. He stood up, shook his head. Faint light glowed through the hole they had dug. A sniff of the air told him that the humans were outside the barn. They were waiting, no doubt, for their chance at the cow. Wolf of Shadows worried a little more meat off a bone. Then the others awoke and lazily ate their fill.

Morning had gone to afternoon when Wolf of Shadows finally left the shelter.

At first his senses were overwhelmed by the increased light of the world. Fields, stones, all were gleaming. It took him a moment to realize that a hazy sun was shining on the ice. Light glowed faintly at the top of the sky, obscured only by thin clouds.

The mother stood shielding her eyes against the light. She raised her face to the sky and cried out.

They were touched by the warmth of the sun, wolf and woman, and he raised his head, too, and howled. His muzzle was filled with scents of deep memory, the saw grass that grew by his puppyhood den, the sweet, heavy smell of his mother, the crunchy taste of the beetles that had been his first kills.

The woman raised her forepaws and sank down, her rear legs bending at the knee. "Sharon, come out here, come see this!"

"Oh, Mother!"

They made the sobbing sound, and it reflected Wolf of Shadow's feeling: a happiness so great it hurt.

The land began to stretch itself, the ice to sigh and crack, and water to drip from the tips of frozen leaves. Wolf of Shadows squinted, and the humans jumped up and down shouting, waving, and the eye of the sun shone down. The other wolves came into the light, also squinting.

The frozen death was gone, and they had survived. Wolf of Shadows could almost smell the clover coming back, and the deer that ran there. A great and nameless emotion settled upon the wolf. He lowered his head and closed his eyes, and the humans beside him did the same, their matted hair agleam in the sunlight. The other wolves came near.

Into him there came the teeming scents of all things that walk and crawl, the creatures that are food for wolves and even those that are not. The urgency of life to be re-born made Wolf of Shadows' very flesh tingle. His impulse was to show his belly to this grand power—and at the same time he wanted to protect it as he would a newly dropped cub.

He heard himself whining as the light flowed about him, reviving the dead land. Then he noticed that the human mother was silent. Her bony forepaws were clutched together, her eyes were tightly shut.

"Please," she said, "please, God, let it stay light. . . ." There followed long, dry rasping sounds from the depths of her shaking body.

Then, just when they were getting used to the light, the storm slammed back with greater fury than ever before. The very air turned to ice. Out of the belly and soul of Wolf of Shadows there came a bitter cry.

The sun had teased them as a yearling does a cub when he snatches a beetle from its clumsy jaws.

The mother came and squatted beside him in the driving snow. She made no sound; neither did her young companion, who rested her naked face against Wolf of Shadows' muzzle.

He did the only thing he knew to do, for his wolves and his humans. He led them forth.

PART FOUR

The Judgment of
the Storm

It may be that some little root of the sacred tree still lives. Nourish it, then, that it may leaf and bloom and fill with singing birds.

Black Elk

M ORE TIME PASSED, many days spent living from a few small kills and some food shells the humans had found, many nights spent huddling together in abandoned human dens. The wolves were thin, the humans like two bunches of twigs, but the pack had developed a rhythm of movement, and they went steadily along.

Then they reached a great river. It was not frozen solid but was rolling with black ice, and impossible to cross. Wolf of Shadows stood staring at it, and his belly churned with anger. The other wolves were lying or sitting around him when the human mother and the young female joined them.

"Mother, it's the Missouri! Has to be."

"How far have we come, Sharon?"

They flailed their long forepaws at each other, enclosed each other. "You're a tough lady, Mother. You've walked seven hundred miles!"

Their voices jingled and they bared their teeth. "Come on, wolves," the young female growled, "now it's your turn to follow us! Don't know a darned thing about bridges, do you?"

The mother tugged at Wolf of Shadows' neck, until at last he went beside her. He moved slowly along at her pace, every so often glaring at the black ice. They continued for a day like that, until there came a place where the land swept up and crossed the water.

They followed it, and stayed a long time on the flat, hard surface that ran endlessly south. Here and there a rolling thing stood abandoned, and from one of them the two humans got some hide-smelling things. Carefully they pulled the tattered hide from their rear paws, drawing it off with much groaning and yelping. Then they attached the new hide-things and seemed much relieved. "We can be glad these people wore our sizes."

"Your size, Momma. I'm dealing with three pair of socks."

Wolf of Shadows would not have liked to have his own paws blinded like that. How could paws understand the ground if they couldn't touch it?

The days of walking on the flat path became a haze of

travel, punctuated by the routine of the occasional kill and the shell food. It was never enough to fill pack bellies but as the way was easier, the wolves were able to pick up speed again. The humans dropped far back, but the wolves remained aware of them, and got into the habit of waiting at the day's end for them to bring food shells and share them around a fire.

Then the routine was broken. Wolf of Shadows had almost forgotten the odor of strange human beings, so completely had his own people become a part of the pack, and so seldom did they now scent living men. A snatch of odor reminded him, though, and then the voices of human males, low and gruff, coming on the wind.

Wolf of Shadows would have altered course to avoid the men, but two of the young wolves chanced upon a dog pack, and took three of them. In the feast that followed, the alien humans were forgotten. Bellies for the moment full, the wolves curled into a pile together. The air was so cold that breath froze against noses and muzzles became stiff with hard ice.

The humans arrived and soon had a fire going. The wolves had learned the sense of lying to the windward side of the flames, and remained there, closed in on themselves. They slept deeply as their bodies digested their first decent meal in days. They did not hear the crunch of approaching boots, nor detect the smell of the two men who suddenly appeared in the light of the campfire.

"Share your fire?"

The mother and her cub reared up, their eyes wide, their mouths dropping open. "Jesus!"

"Hey, take it easy. We're not spooks."

Wolf of Shadows reacted to the fear of his humans by flattening his ears against his head. He made no sound.

"Where'd you come from? Who are you?"

"Take it easy, ma'am. We won't hurt you." The two strangers hunched over the fire, their backs to the wind. "Been a long day. We've been hoping to find another farm, but it's slow going on foot. Had a Toyota four-wheel-drive wagon, but there's no electricity to get gas out of the pumps. We've been walking for about ten days, I think."

"All the cars we've seen have had frozen batteries."

Wolf of Shadows turned one ear back, trying to take meaning from the tone of the growls. He opened his eyes but did not move.

"What you got here, some kinda dog team?"

"Yeah, a dog team." Wolf of Shadows raised his head. The mother's voice quavered. His impulse was to rush the invaders, but then he smelled death-sticks. He remained motionless.

"Looks like a couple of hundred pounds of meat on them dogs. They trained? Hunt? Pull a sled?"

"They hunt."

"Hey, you're scared. Isn't she scared, Mr. Jackson?"

"Scared, Mike."

Wolf of Shadows was not the only member of the pack who had heard and smelled. They remained still, listening, noses twitching.

"You do real well for yourselves, nature girls. You're wearing parkas, you got new boots and these dogs—you raised in the woods or something?"

"I'm an animal ethologist. I'm—or I was—with the University of Minnesota."

One of the men moved. "Look, I guess I'll just say this straight out. You gotta give us everything you have. Boots, parkas, even those dogs."

"You'll let us freeze?"

"Either you or our wives and kids! I got four children in a trailer somewhere back there, and they're dying. We got nothing left. Those dogs are gold. Even if they won't hunt for us, they're fresh meat. Either we shoot you and take what you got, or you give it to us. It's your call."

Wolf of Shadows stood up during this particularly long growl. This was some kind of a challenge, he sensed it.

"The one that just got to his feet," the young female said, "he's the team leader. You've got to put a collar around his neck. The others will follow."

"Mike, I think those are wolves."

"No, Mr. Jackson, they are not wolves. Have you got a collar, lady?"

"Your web belt will do."

Wolf of Shadows watched with growing astonishment as the man laid his death-stick on the ground, took part of his covering off and turned it into a vine-thing, and then came forward, his teeth bared in open challenge. "Here, dog, here now. Easy, dog! What's his name?"

"Black."

"Okay, Black—"

Wolf of Shadows had no choice. It was a challenge and it could not be ignored. He leaped past the out-stretched paws and bit at the throat.

There was hardly a struggle. The man was weak. He reared back, his forepaws clutching wildly. Then the pack attacked and there was confusion. The other man began waving his arms and barking, his voice a babble.

Then a death-stick was pointing at Wolf of Shadows.

The great wolf did the only thing he could. His heart thundering, his mind whirling with images of torn and dying wolves, he grabbed the monstrous thing in his jaws, his teeth clanging against the coldness of it. He pulled it so hard that it flew free of the man's hands, fell to the ground, and made a loud, flashing bark. Instead of dying, it leaped into the hands of the other man, pointed again, and kept barking. But by then the wolves had all melted into the dark.

For a moment the only sounds were the clicking of the death-stick and the gasping of the wounded man.

"Dogs, hell, lady! Those are wolves!"

"They're our friends. And if you keep shooting that thing you might get one or two, but the others will tear you to pieces before you can get them all."

"Wolves! And you—they—" His voice stopped.

"My daughter and I don't control these wolves. We're members of their pack. The big black that nearly killed you is our leader."

The two men moved back away from the fire, slipping into the night without a further sound.

The days passed without counting, a seasonless twilight of ice and brutal wind. The sleet changed slowly to hard-grained snow and then to ice as fine as sand. The cold clutched them more and more tightly. Whenever Wolf of Shadows thought it could not get worse the wind rose again and the ice seemed to penetrate not only his fur but his skin, and finally his bones and blood.

The pack went blindly on. Some of them had lost toes and parts of their ears. Their noses were cracked and dry, and every breath meant pain. The shell food, always scarce, had all but disappeared. Most of the shells the humans were finding were empty or burst.

Some of the pack—one female and the human mother—lost teeth. All of them had lost some fur, and the wind was savage against bare skin. They had sores to lick but little strength to lick them. When they stopped to rest, they curled into themselves as they had when they were very young. The humans now burrowed in the pack just like wolves, reaching out only to tend the pack's night fire. Like the wolves the humans were wisps of things, all bony angles and great hollow eyes. The mother's breath was ragged, and the young female whimpered in her sleep.

Wolf of Shadows had become very close to the mother. He considered that he now had two mates, the beautiful wolf he shared with the gray, and this one, who was a mate of the heart.

He licked her forepaws and she put her face close to his. He was used to her growling ritual, which he endured patiently, sometimes making sense of the emotions she conveyed, sometimes not. "You know what the difference is between wolves and men? Each of you is all of you— pack and species. And you know it, and take your love of one another from it. Before the war people became so separate from one another we were like leaves in the sea. We were alone."

She made a sound then that seemed to rise out of a cave within her, it was so deep. He could not even whimper consolation to such a tone.

* * *

Plodding across the black ice, avoiding now even the most faint scent of alien humans, Wolf of Shadows came to a time when he began to think there was no south, and that there would never be another bit of living game.

The plains changed to hills and the hills to mountains. Ghost forests covered the mountains, and winds roared through the sky as the washes of spring once roared down the streams.

The wolves never trotted now, but rather walked. At night the humans would lay their paws upon the wolves' ears and send delicious tingles down them with rubbing softer than the softest lick.

The pack had spent the night at a ruined human den and was struggling up yet another mountain when Wolf of Shadows noticed a change. He looked back to see a young male and four females sitting down. The gray, his mate, one young wolf, and another female remained with him. The two humans also clambered up the ice.

Wolf of Shadows went back to the malingerers and made the largest of them roll. Then he started out again. This time only the gray and their mate came with him. The rest of the pack moved away from them, back toward the ruined den. It contained bones gnawed by dogs. Maybe twenty humans had died there. The mother and her cub had rejoiced to find food shells, and all had eaten the salted mud that had appeared in them when they were put near a fire.

His wolves had to be encouraged. He cavorted, he threatened by showing his teeth. They whined and lowered their tails. He ran a little way ahead, jumping in the ice, forcing himself to wave his own tail confidently.

Still they hung back, their eyes suffering his humiliation with him. When he detected their sour, heavy odor, he realized that nothing would convince them to come. It wasn't a lack of faith in him. On the contrary, their eyes were filled with faith, but their bodies were exhausted. One of the females licked a shattered paw. Another attended her scraggly pelt, whimpering.

His mate trotted over to them. Wolf of Shadows glared at her. She of all wolves must not abandon him. When he growled at her she lowered her tail.

It was the gray who decided for both of them. The old leader stood shoulder to shoulder with Wolf of Shadows.

Their mate came back. The rest of the little troupe trotted away through the gloom, and soon disappeared, going back toward the broken den. Even now unwilling to accept defeat, Wolf of Shadows ran after them. They were his wolves. He could not leave them to die!

Just once, the gray whined at him. Wolf of Shadows lowered his tail and forced himself to accept the gray's meaning: He could not mend broken strength. As he left he heard his poor wolves tearing at the miserable bones in the den, snarling among themselves. His heart beating sadness, he returned to what remained of his pack: the gray, their mate, and the two scrawny human beings.

They continued up the mountain, through what once had been a pine forest, but which was now gloomy and dark, the trees almost buried in ice and snow, and nothing alive at all. There was not even the scent of death here.

His body ached the more not to feel the pack with him, not to have the wind at his face and a long string of wolves behind. He fought the urge to turn around, to forget his quest, to go back and be with them in the shelter, gnawing bones and waiting for the long sleep.

The wind snatched at him; the snow pounded against him. He lowered his head and blinked the ice away from his eyes. His freezing paws cracked against the icy ground and his fur was so matted that it hardly kept out the cold at all.

One night in the dark fastness of the mountains, he scented a familiar wolf: his own mother. She was as huge as she had been when he was a cub, a flesh-and-blood creature, her teats dripping with milk, her belly warm and soft, another cub cuddled there. He went to her, pressed his head into the soft underflesh of her, and felt her milk in his throat. He and the other cub drank until their bellies were full.

Wolf of Shadows saw that the huge female was all white, as white as death, and knew her for who she really was. And did not care.

Then he was jolted awake by the young human. The huge female became a frozen boulder, her teat a bit of ice. He jumped back in surprise and horror, for next to the boulder lay the frozen body of another great wolf, nursing there, long dead. He sniffed the ruined wolf and looked upon the famished lips, the teeth caught in a final snarl of agony, the black tongue. The cold had captured a portrait of death: the eyes forever glistening, the nose forever wrinkled in a last, desperate scenting of dead air.

Here was a brother, another lone wolf, one who had not had anyone to awaken him from the dream of death.

Wolf of Shadows walked on, moving carefully on his cracked paws. His mate and his gray were no faster, and the humans were at last no slower. All moved with the angular grace of the starving, mincing delicately along in the ice.

When they lay down that night, the young female took his head in her lap and stroked his ears. She had made a fire, and they were blessed with its blowing flames, a little warmth against the relentless cutting weather. The gray and their mate lay beside him, whimpering. The human mother was next to them.

Morning came, and with it aching bones and bellies so empty that the wolves moaned. Wolf of Shadows' flesh was dry and withered, his skin rubbed raw where his ribs chafed. He looked at the humans, two slow shadows. It was good to feel them near and to smell their smells.

He took a breath, scenting little in the caked, crackling misery of his muzzle. He tried to rise but could not. Every part of him hurt. The worst place was the tip of his nose, which felt as if it were being pierced by quills every time he drew a breath. Had the other wolves been of greater courage, to face the ice with calm hearts? He wanted to howl but did not have the strength.

"Don't you dare die, wolf." The young human wrapped her forelegs around his neck and pressed her face against his own. Her breath was hot, her voice deep with strength. "We have to keep going. Everything is dead, wolf, except you and me and the other three. There aren't even any houses in these mountains, and no cans of food. We have a responsibility to live, wolf." Wolf of Shadows sensed something like the courage of the yearling beneath the hooves of the moose, or the cub struggling for the first time to raise its head.

And then there was the ice and the wind.

"I don't think he's going to get up, Mother."

"Can you blame him?"

"Did we come this far just to die? We could have accomplished that a long time ago."

The two humans curled around each other, wrapping themselves in their hides. Ice blew in drifts around the frail group. The wolves nuzzled into what warmth remained in their bodies. Human paws twined in their soft underfur, and backs were turned to the storm.

When Wolf of Shadows woke, he found the humans curled up with the wolves. He licked the frozen paws of the mother, and the gray licked the young female, who awoke and made sounds like a brook running. "He's tickling me, Mother."

"I love you, wolves," whispered the mother.

Wolf of Shadows heard the emotion in her tones. He wished he could sniff out some food to reward his pack's loyalty.

The young female's paws came around his neck. "I wish I could make you warm," she said.

The storm roared. The snow changed to sleet. Sleep again overcame them all.

When Wolf of Shadows woke again, it was from a dream of snuffling in green ferns. He gradually became aware of how cold he was, with ice crusting his back. Only his nose, cupped in a human forepaw, was really warm. He did not know how long he had slept, but he knew that he felt a little stronger. The custom of sharing warmth had kept them all alive.

The wolves got up and shook themselves. The humans tumbled in the ice they threw off, both chattering like angry squirrels.

Wolf of Shadows set off, followed by the gray and their mate. The humans took their place at the rear. For a time the pack moved in single file. Then the gray and the female trotted off ahead to hunt.

Soon the two of them began to move faster. Then Wolf of Shadows smelled it too—the scent of living flesh!

"Oh, God, they're speeding up."

"Just keep moving, Mother."

They trudged forward. He watched the mother's body jerk and shake in the wind, heard the flapping of her skins. When she cried, the young female encouraged her.

The gray and their mate had stopped on the brow of a hill, and Wolf of Shadows trotted up to join them. What he saw made him tremble with eagerness. Three small, emaciated deer were nuzzling the ice that filled a little mountain valley.

How beautiful they looked, how sweet they smelled. Wolf of Shadows grew very still, taking the measure of the hunt. To charge them—that was the thing. They would run up the little canyon and get caught in the snow. They would never climb out in time.

There wasn't a moment to waste—deer ears were turning, deer noses twitching. Wolf of Shadows trotted closer. He listened to their breathing, to the sound of their hooves in the ice, and to the crackle of the frozen weeds they were chewing. He drew their scent into his muzzle, analyzing the odor as best he could for signs of fear or alarm. And he watched them, three hazy shadows in the dark land.

His two wolves fanned out to either side of him. All advanced on the deer, moving with the utmost stealth. They were afraid, because all knew that this was a final effort. It was eat or die. Wolf of Shadows felt as heavy as if his fur were soaked. He had once flown on strong legs. Now he trotted, unwilling to break into a run until absolutely necessary.

He drew closer to the deer. He could see their eyes looking up and down the canyon, see their ears turning this way and that. They pawed at the ground, sticking their noses into the ice. He drooled. His hunger was a blood taste in the back of his mouth, charging him with desire.

They crept closer. The rangy little buck turned its ears toward the gray. Its head rose. Then it blew, flicked its tail, and began a clattering run across the ice. It went right up to the end of the canyon, followed by its family.

Wolf nails rattled, and the three of them were off, dragging tired bodies forward, the succulent scent of the deer in their nostrils. They ran up the canyon, until the terrified animals were a jump away.

Suddenly the impossible happened. As if granted flight, the three deer leaped over the wolves and began bounding down toward the open end of the canyon and freedom.

The wolves turned, frantically snapping. They chased the deer down the canyon. Wolf of Shadows plunged into snowbanks, clawing, grabbing, forcing himself forward. He skittered on ice, fell and tumbled, ran furiously, his muzzle questing, getting closer, almost touching the rump of a doe, then falling a nose back. His breath came hard, catching in his throat, the cold searing his nose, and he fell farther back. With a great rush and crash of frozen brush the deer climbed the very bank from which the wolves had first spotted them, and in an instant were gone.

Wolf of Shadows stood at the bottom of the bank. Then he saw, rising on the top of the hill the deer were climbing, a familiar figure. It waved its forepaws and shouted, pounded its rear paws on the ground, and jerked up and down, looking like a gigantic, flapping crow in the snow, with its shrieking mother beside it.

His wolves were with him now, breathing hard, and the sounds of the deer were getting louder as they turned away from the humans, only to find themselves facing the wolves. Their own slowness had put the humans in exactly the right place. Some of the old joy of the hunt returned, and Wolf of Shadows felt renewed strength.

In their terror the deer blew and kicked. One of them sailed out into the air directly over the female. She leaped high, her tail corkscrewing, her body twisting, her muzzle reaching, and caught the creature's ankle in her jaws. The contact lasted only an instant but it was enough. The deer's jump was broken and it fell with a dry crash into the bottom of the canyon.

Even as the gray's mate leaped on it, the creature got up and managed to scurry away. But Wolf of Shadows and the gray cornered another of the animals. The gray bravely got under its belly, dodging the frantic hooves, and nipped open its guts as Wolf of Shadows attacked its throat, grabbing the thin neck with his teeth. The deer hardly gasped, and then was dead.

The third one escaped by rushing the humans, who were far too slow to catch it. They deserved their lives, this tough little buck and the doe that had escaped. No doubt they had also been seeking the sun, the buck guiding its little herd south.

Deer flesh was scattered about. The three wolves gobbled, hardly noticing the arrival of the humans. The two of them squatted three leaps away. The mother worked at a fire, grunting and struggling, while Wolf of Shadows filled his belly with glorious food, and felt the strength of it begin to course through his exhausted body. The young female came forward, the silver claw in her forepaw. She set about cutting away some of the meat. The wolves did not stop her. The humans had earned their place at the kill. This time they did not have to wait.

"That's a lovely fire, Mother."

"Your old mother's learned a thing or two about making a fire. Hurry up and skin that haunch so we can cook it."

After he was done, Wolf of Shadows went to the fire. He sat with the others at the edge of its light, his coat steaming. The wolves curled up together while the humans burned the life out of their meat and ate it. "Members of a wolf pack. Who would have believed it?"

"If we weren't in the pack we'd be dead. That's what counts, Mother."

Night passed swiftly in the canyon. Far overhead the

wind shrieked, but few gusts reached down into this shelter. The fire burned low, and finally became embers. The pack slept heavily, disappearing slowly beneath the snow.

A thin dawn spread down the rocks. The sky remained dark gray. The wolves stretched themselves and licked at ice. With much groaning and protest, the humans also arose. Soon Wolf of Shadows again felt the call south. There was nothing to keep them here; their kill had been so pitifully thin, its flesh had all been eaten in the first gorging.

The thought of moving almost made Wolf of Shadows curl up again, but he forced himself to rise. He started off, just managing to trot. As he went along he raised his tail and wagged it to encourage the others. The pack began to struggle up the walls of the canyon.

When they reached the sloping surface of the mountainside the wind hit them, and the female howled miserably. She had lost much of her underfur. Her belly was naked, the skin black. The humans scurried along behind, breathing hard with the effort to keep up.

The pack moved through another featureless day, cresting the highest ridges of the mountains and starting down. They traveled carefully. A fall would mean a broken bone and certain death.

Soon the darkness began to close around them again. When Wolf of Shadows sat down, the rest of them dropped. He snuffled the others, and began licking the human mother. They all ate snow, then gnawed some deer bones the humans had brought.

As night fell the sleet stopped.

"Sharon—"

"I know, Mother."

"Do you think it's clearing?"

"No, Mother."

The dark itself seemed to be watching them, somehow judging them as a mother judges her wriggling litter, separating out the weak.

Wolves and humans twined close. In the middle of the dark, silence began to replace the ceaseless wind. It dropped and dropped until at last there was nothing but the ping of ice. Then there was not even that. The quiet made them all alert.

"Sharon, what's happening?"

Wolf of Shadows searched the blackness, for he had scented a vanishing odor, a freshness he associated with living plants.

The smell disappeared. Perhaps it had never been there. He closed his eyes. Half sleeping, he dreamed. In his dream he found his lost wolves. Their fur was matted no more and their bellies were full, and in their eyes was contentment. The pack was together again, for their leader had brought them through.

Then he was awake. There was no smell of fresh plant life, of grass and leaves. In the face of his memories Wolf of Shadows felt himself a humble creature, a bit of fur and bone and a beating heart. His tail touched the ground.

"The air feels damp, Mother, not frozen, but damp."

"I don't want to hope."

There came restless sighing in the sky, then the wind came back so hard that the pack, wolves and humans, were rolled in the freezing, stinging sleet. Thunder tore the air, ice came in a cataract, and the wind sang higher and higher. The little clutch of creatures sought one another. The wind was so fierce that even their huddle could not shelter them.

This was the judgment of the storm. It went on mercilessly all the rest of the night and through the blind morning. For the first time in their long journey they couldn't move at all, not in this whipping torrent of sleet. When afternoon brought an end to it, they were nothing but a shapeless mass, hardly more than a fold in the ground.

But they were alive, and they were not frozen.

They were wet. Wolf of Shadows looked up. The gray looked up, and the female. The humans stirred.

"Mother, the sleet's turning to rain!"

Then the sky lifted from the land, revealing a long view down the mountains. In the southerly valleys, here and there, were patches where the ice had melted. Wolf of Shadows got to his feet. He was so tired he could hardly walk, but they had to move when they could. They could still make some progress before dark.

He heard flowing water.

Was it warmer below?

He raised his head, then wagged his tail and trotted on. Grumbling and slipping, his pack followed him down.

Would there be a place for them in the valleys, where at last they might rest?

Wolves and humans together, they set off to find out.

AFTERWORD

❧

AFTER WRITING *Warday* with Jim Kunetka, I got a large number of letters, some expressing opinions or ideas for peace, some asking questions. Most of these letters were from young people, just as most of our call-in questioners on radio and television programs throughout the world were under the age of twenty-five.

One letter in particular touched me deeply, and opened up my mind to a new level of thinking about the crisis of human aggression that characterizes our era. It was from a young woman, and she asked the question, "What about the animals?" She added, "Because we can end the world, we have responsibility for it, and it is not just human life that matters, but helpless life, too."

So I tried to write a book that would express the plight of helpless life which, after the terrible war, also includes humanity. The wolves and their human companions can only struggle and hope.

Men and wolves do not now have the kind of relationship that I portray in *Wolf of Shadows*. It is conjectural, based on research, my own personal experience of wolves, and knowledge of Native American ways of viewing the wolf, which are so different from the modern image of wolves as vicious enemies of man. The bond that develops between the wolves and the human beings in the story is meant to suggest that we can find new ways of thinking about, and relating to, animals. We assume that animals are lower beings because they cannot manipulate nature as we do. Is this true? Perhaps another truth, suggested by traditional Native American wisdom, is also valid: that there is something sacred present in animals which deserves notice and respect.

I cannot say whether or not Wolf of Shadows ever finds his pack a warm valley, because that is not the true end of the story. Nobody knows exactly what will happen if someone turns on the nuclear death machine we have installed on our planet.

The true end of the story comes when we decide, as a species, to dismantle the machine and use our great intelligence on behalf of the earth that bears us, instead of against her.

WHITLEY STRIEBER is the co-author of *Warday* and author of *The Wolfen* and *The Hunger*. He was born and raised in San Antonio, Texas, and now lives with his wife and son in New York City. He has studied and tracked wild wolves in northern Minnesota, the lake country described in *Wolf of Shadows*.

Gulf of Mexico

5 megatons

2 megatons

ATLANTIC OCEAN

3 megatons

4 megatons

Tennessee   River

Mississippi River

2 megatons

4 megatons

APPALACHIAN MOUNTAINS

Ohio   River

4 megatons

6 megatons

8 megatons

3 megatons

18 megatons

Lake Erie

3 megatons

15 megatons

2 megatons

Lake Ontario

Lake Michigan

3 megator

Lake Huron

2 megatons

Lake Superior